"I'm looking for Bolan told the

"First you shoot me, then you ask for favors? What's in it for me?"

"Some mercy," Bolan said simply.

"Let me live," D'Andrea countered, "and I'll tell you what I know. But I want your word."

The big warrior smiled. "You got it."

There was a pause, and Bolan thought the mobster had a change of heart, but the voice creaked out again and uttered a name.

D'Andrea could see the Beretta's silenced muzzle homing on his groin, and he read his doom on Bolan's face.

"Hey, you promised," the mafioso cried.

"I lied," the Executioner said. And squeezed the trigger.

Twice.

MACK BOLAN

The Executioner

DON PENDLETON's EXECUTIONER
MACK BOLAN
Hollywood Hell

A GOLD EAGLE BOOK FROM

TORONTO · NEW YORK · LONDON · PARIS
AMSTERDAM · STOCKHOLM · HAMBURG
ATHENS · MILAN · TOKYO · SYDNEY

First edition May 1985

ISBN 0-373-61077-7

Special thanks and acknowledgment to
Mike Newton for his contributions to this work.

Printed in Canada

To the anguished parents
of today's runaways.
Someone is doing something.

Strike—till the last armed foe expires;
Strike—for your altars and your fires;
Strike—for the green graves of your sires;
God—and your native land.
      —*Fitz-Green Halleck: Marco Bozzaris*

He conquers who endures.
                              —*Persius* A.D. *34–62*

PROLOGUE

The darkness faded and two giant figures sprang into sharp focus upon the makeshift screen. A man and woman, nude, lay intertwined on a rumpled bed, pretending not to notice lights and camera as they copulated listlessly. Their movements were devoid of passion, and the heavy breathing that was meant to pass for sound effects did nothing to arouse their two-man audience.

"That's Julie Price," the younger of the men said. He made no attempt to hide his evident distaste for the performance they were viewing.

"Who's the stud?" Mack Bolan asked, his full attention focused on the faces now, ignoring panoramic shots of heaving, sweating bodies.

"No name yet," his young companion answered. "I've been working on it, but names don't mean much in this business. Faces, either, when you come right down to it. Not all of these so-called actors work through agencies."

The Executioner could buy that, sure. It took a certain kind of agent to subsist on selling human flesh like so much produce in a supermarket. Some of them were listed in the trades, of course, but for the rest you had to have experience at searching under stones.

"I'll need a name," he said unnecessarily.

On the screen five more figures crowded around the bed. They were all male, surrounding and devouring the woman with their bodies. Bolan had a flash impression that she might be drowning, and for just a heartbeat, as she faced the camera, there was something that he recognized behind her eyes.

A look of desperation.

"Is this the film they showed her father?" Bolan asked.

"One of them. I've got some others, but they're pretty much the same."

"Let's kill it, Johnny."

With a single motion, Bolan's companion turned off the projector, keyed the lights and drove the naked giants back into their shadow world of limbo. Neither man was sorry to be rid of them.

Mack Bolan lit a cigarette and waited for the smoke to clear his palate of the sour taste that had developed in his mouth. Irrationally, he had a sudden urge to wash his hands.

Across the table Bolan's brother, Johnny, watched the big man silently and waited, knowing he would speak when he was ready.

"Looks like standard blackmail," Bolan said at length. "How's your client handling it?"

"He came to me. That's something."

Bolan nodded. Something, yes. But what?

"How well do you know Foster Price?"

"I met him through the storefront office, worked with him on this and that. I'd read him as sincere, committed. Solid senatorial material."

"Which makes him valuable," Bolan finished for him.

"Right. To both sides."

Personally, Bolan had little use for politics and politicians. He had seen too many of them sell their souls for some ready cash or the promise of their secret fantasies fulfilled. And while he did not brand them all as worthless and corrupt, he preferred to take their campaign promises with several grains of salt.

The soldier was impressed. He valued Johnny's instincts. If he thought that Foster Price was worth the effort it might cost to save him, then it might be something for the Executioner to look into.

"Last address on the daughter?" Bolan asked.

"So far, just Hollywood."

The young man read his brother's weary look and spread his hands.

"I'm working on it, Mack. I've still got the producers left to check, directors, casting agents that I might've missed..."

"Keep after it," the soldier told him. "Maybe I can find a shortcut once I'm on the scene."

It took a moment for the words to register, and then the younger Bolan smiled.

"We'll take it, then?" he asked.

"It's worth a look," the Executioner replied. "If Price is all the man you think he is..."

"I'm betting on it."

That was good enough for Bolan—at the moment. He could make a battlefield assessment of the situation later, when he had more hard intelligence. But right now there was that other thing.

The girl.

Those hurting eyes had reached out and locked with Bolan's for a broken heartbeat, pleading with him. He would find her if he could, and help her if it was within his power.

Bolan closed his eyes and saw the pleading face again, emblazoned on the inside of his eyelids like some kind of laser-blast tattoo. The face was new to him but he was only too familiar with the painful look it bore.

The Executioner would carry that pain with him into Hollywood, and it would make him strong. For Johnny. For the pleading woman-child. For justice, right.

And he was carrying the fire back to his enemies once more. Still hot enough to scorch them where they clustered in their holes and tunnels, hiding from the purifying light of day. Mack Bolan meant to drag them out and let them see the light they had been hiding from for so long.

The Executioner was coming, right, and he was carrying the fire. He hoped that Hollywood could stand the heat.

1

The studio was one of those exclusive homes you find along Topanga Canyon, built to give the feel of "roughing it" on several manicured acres west of Los Angeles proper. The place had not been occupied with any regularity for two years now, although it was not quite abandoned.

Rather, it had taken on a new utility. Once a home of stars and would-be stars, it had become a place where stars were born...at least in theory.

Although the cameras had been rolling night and day for nearly eighteen months, to the best of Bolan's knowledge no Academy Award material was ever filmed inside those walls. Instead, a different kind of product was being churned out, the sort of films that even the "adult arcades" might find too hot to handle. Sadomasochism, child pornography, a touch of bestiality, perhaps. At one time or another Bolan's information told him that it all had happened inside those brooding walls.

It was a place to start, no more, no less.

He had no solid intel linking Julie Price with any of the films produced there, but the distribution outlets that had retailed some of her films also handled movies cranked out at the studio.

The men who ran those distribution outlets, shipping their cargoes full of human degradation nationwide, were well connected with the local Mafia.

And that was more than just a starting point.

With any luck at all, it just might carry Bolan to first base, and from there... The warrior cleared his mind deliberately, blotting out the forecasts as he concentrated on the here and now.

The outer wall had been no problem for him. Bolan had scaled it easily, and saw no guards around the wrought-iron gates in front.

Once inside, the soldier hit a combat crouch, becoming one with darkness as he let his senses probe the night around him. He was looking for an enemy, a trap—some sign that he, or someone like him, was expected by the quarry.

And he came up empty.

They were used to privacy up here, the soldier knew. Once upon a time, back in the bad old Manson days when paranoia was the rule, he might have found sophisticated listening devices festooning the estate grounds...but not tonight.

Los Angeles had grown complacent once again, and old fears were forgotten like the tremors of the last big earthquake.

Mack Bolan was more than grateful for small favors. If his targets felt secure it would be that much easier to reach them, and the warrior never minded shortcuts if they got him where he meant to go.

And back again. Oh, yes. The most important part was getting out alive.

Most important, sure, and many times the hardest part.

The Executioner was rigged for combat, hoping at the same time that he would not need the hardware that he wore as a precaution. Hands and face were blackened by the special goo that let him merge with shadows, and the midnight skinsuit fit him like a second layer of flesh. Beneath his arm, the silenced Beretta 93-R was nestled in its special harness. Big Thunder, the .44 AutoMag, rode Bolan's hip on military webbing, and the canvas pouches that encircled his waist held extra magazines for both his chosen side arms. Hidden pockets in the skinsuit held their own surprises—slim stilettos, razor-fine garrotes made from piano wire—the sundry tools of Bolan's martial trade.

That trade was death, but he was interested in life this night, as well. This was a soft probe designed to gather the intelligence that he would need to reach the next phase of his Hollywood campaign.

The Executioner had satisfied himself that he was alone in the darkness, and he left his hiding place against the wall, a gliding shadow moving in and out among the trees.

The man-made woods were more than adequate for Bolan's needs. They gave him cover as he crossed the several hundred yards between the low retaining wall and the house, which squatted well back from the highway. The latest tenants valued privacy as much as anyone along the canyon, and with better reason.

The soldier wondered for a moment what the neighbors might say or do if they knew about the misery enacted behind those walls.

No matter, he thought. Forget about the neighbors. There was someone on the scene ready to act if necessary. Ready, yes, and willing.

Bolan saw the floodlights through the trees before he saw the house itself. As he approached he found the grounds around the mansion ablaze from spotlights mounted on the corners of the sloping roof.

Whatever might be going on in there, the momentary tenants wanted light enough to see if any uninvited company should try to cross the final fifty yards of vacant lawn between the house and Bolan's own position among the trees.

It was going to be a bitch, that final fifty yards . . . but he had to try it.

The warrior was about to move, deciding on a lateral angle of attack that would afford him the protection of the trees as long as possible, when movement downrange changed his mind. Two men emerged from what appeared to be a kitchen entrance, pausing on the doorstep to check out the night around them, finally moving toward a carport in the rear. Two Lincoln Continentals waited there, and one slid behind the wheel of each, big engines firing to life instantly.

They brought the cars up to the side door, parked them one behind the other. Bolan waited, watching as the door was opened once again, disgorging other bodies. He had counted four before one of them captured the warrior's complete attention.

The fifth man out was struggling, a guard on either side as they forced him toward the cars. His efforts were hampered by the fact that his hands were bound behind his back. Despite his best attempts to make a break for it, they held him easily.

Too far away to make out faces, but Bolan did not need to know the hostage. Right now it was enough to know that he existed, that his captors plainly meant him harm. They might be taking him to more secure prison quarters or conveying him to death and secret burial somewhere among the canyons.

Either way, Bolan meant to interrupt their party.

And soft probes had a way of going hard, damn right. He could forget about the battlefield intelligence for now...at least until he finished with the exercise at hand.

It was an exercise in pure survival—for Bolan and the hostage. If he succeeded, then they had a chance, and he might have gained access to a source of valuable information. If he blew it...

Bolan realized the grim alternative to victory, but he was not prepared to entertain the thought. Not while there was still an opportunity to complete his coup successfully.

It would require audacity together with the slim advantage of surprise he still maintained.

Another rapid head count made it ten men total, including the drivers. The men were split between the Lincolns, with their hostage in the point car, sandwiched between two hardmen on the rear seat.

There was no further movement from the house to indicate that they were leaving anyone behind, but Bolan could not take the risk of moving against them here, where other guns and watching eyes might be concealed, prepared to riddle him before he cleared the trees.

The Executioner retraced his footsteps through the woods, running parallel to the curving driveway, heading in the general direction of the gate. There was a sweeping turn not too far ahead, he remembered, where cars and crews would be completely screened by trees from any watchers in the house.

Behind him, Bolan heard the Lincolns pulling out, tires crunching gravel as they gained momentum, moving single file along the driveway. It would be close, he knew, and he was fairly sprinting now, intent on keeping his appointment with the miniconvoy.

Another few yards with branches whipping at his face and tugging at his nightsuit and he would make it.

Bolan cleared the trees, almost stumbling down the short slope toward the driveway where it began to curve. No sign yet of the Lincolns, and he had the silver AutoMag clutched in his fist before the sound of revving engines reached him, closing fast.

The point car rumbled into view, and it was alone. The second Lincoln was nowhere to be seen.

Bolan did a frantic double take, assuming that the second crew had been delayed somehow, called back to the house...anything. He responded with the lightning instincts of a lifelong combat veteran, letting reflex take over from conscious volition.

The flash grenade was in his hand before the Continental's driver recognized his danger. Bolan ripped the pin free, dropped the spoon and with the tank at twenty yards he pitched a strike directly at the broad expanse of tinted windshield.

The wheelman was reacting now, but too late as he slowed the crew wagon, not ready to commit himself until he got his orders from the hardman riding shotgun. But by the time those orders came it was too late for any meaningful reaction at the wheel.

The flash grenade bounced once across the Lincoln's hood and detonated almost in the driver's startled face. Downrange the Executioner averted his eyes, relying on the distance and deflection of the blast to save him from the shock waves that were generated by the stun-bomb. He felt the momentary wind whip past him, and the heartbeat flare of noonday had already faded to darkness when he swiveled toward the confrontation.

The Lincoln's driver had lost it in the explosion. One hand across his eyes, the guy was steering blind, trying to correct his drift. The other gunners had been likewise blinded, deafened by the stunning blast, and they were clinging to the nearest handhold as their vehicle was suddenly transformed into a roller coaster.

Bolan watched the Lincoln as it veered across the two-lane driveway, swerving, finally climbing the embankment he had scrambled down a moment earlier. The radials were losing traction in the loose earth, and great plumes of dirt and gravel were spewing up behind the Continental as it dug a trench into the hillside.

The Executioner was closing, hammer back on the AutoMag, before the first man scrambled out and tried to make his break. Half-blinded as he was, the thug had managed to pull iron from a hidden harness, waving a .45 in front of himself, probing for a target he would never find.

Big Thunder spoke then, a single awesome word, and pieces of the gunner's skull were outward-bound before he knew that he was dead. His body vaulted backward, driven by 240 grains of righteous fury, then rebounded off the snarling Lincoln.

Other doors were springing open on the Continental now, and armed hardmen were emerging slightly unprepared to confront the faceless enemy. Three side arms cracked almost in unison, but the gunners were feeling for a target, searching for the echo of Bolan's own artillery, their aching eyes not fit yet for the kind of pinpoint shooting they would need to stay alive.

The Executioner let them hear the AutoMag, unloading three rounds from left to right in rapid-fire. And he was firing for effect. Three up, three down, and the thugs were scattering like punctured combat silhouettes, empty scarecrow figures reeling out of frame and out of mind as Bolan closed in on his target.

One gunner left, behind the wheel, and this one was still fighting with the gearshift, thinking he could make it work despite the fact that he was axle-deep in dirt and clearly going nowhere. From the corner of an aching eye he saw Grim Death approaching and knew that he was running out of time. A final burst of frenzied energy, a clawing for the holstered weapon he could never hope to reach, and then his world fell in around him.

The silver cannon bucked in Bolan's fist, its foot-long tongue of muzzle flame reaching out to lap against the driver's window. And the screaming face behind the glass was changing now, imploding, disappearing into crimson mist. Dead fingers froze around a holstered side arm, locked there for an impotent eternity before the headless mannequin collapsed across the seat.

The Executioner was moving swiftly, circling the killing ground in search of life. He found it in the back seat of the Continental, huddled against the floorboards, waiting for the storm around him to pass away.

The hostage flinched as Bolan placed a firm hand on his shoulder. The narrow eyes that scanned his face and fastened on the AutoMag were bright, alert, undamaged by the flash grenade. The Executioner surmised that this one's captors must have forced him to lie down behind the front seat as they left the house, attempting to conceal him from the view of passersby once they were off the property and running clear.

So much for planning, right.

"Who are you? What...?" the hostage inquired tremulously.

"No time for twenty questions now," the warrior told him. "I'm a friend. Believe it. And we've got to go. Right now."

As if to emphasize his words, the tardy second Lincoln chose that moment to appear around the curve uprange, its high beams tunneling the darkness, locking for an instant on Mack Bolan as he stood behind the stricken point car.

The second Continental, with its complement of guns, was bearing down upon them, gaining speed, big headlights eating up the night like hungry eyes. Once the hunter, Mack Bolan had become the hunted, and he reacted with the grim ferocity of any jungle predator at bay.

He *moved*, damn right, and God help anyone who barred his way.

2

Bolan swiveled to confront the threat, Big Thunder up and tracking into target acquisition as his finger tightened on the trigger. He held the cannon steady and snapped off a stunning double-punch at thirty yards, and was rewarded by the sound of glass exploding and the shriek of tortured rubber on the pavement.

Uprange, the driver died with his foot on the brake, one last reflexive action that put the Continental through a screaming half turn, lurching to a stop as the tank stalled. Wheelman number two, his face splattered against the driver's window, had made his final pit stop.

But there were other guns there, each reacting swiftly to the sudden, unexpected danger. They were exiting the Lincoln, keeping it between them and the Executioner, seeking cover behind the big crew wagon as they unlimbered their weapons.

Bolan did not plan to wait around and let them take their time picking out a target. He was already moving swiftly when the Lincoln found its resting place among the trees. He dumped the AutoMag's expended magazine and snapped a new one into place, the movements automatic. The soldier's mind was on his enemies—and on the man he had taken such great risks to rescue from their hands.

The hostage had apparently decided he would trust Bolan, to a point. Despite the bonds around his wrists, the man had made his own way from the Lincoln. On turning briefly from his confrontation with the chase car, Bolan found him crouching in the darkness near the body of a fallen gunner.

"This way," Bolan snapped, and jerked his head in the direction of the darkened trees.

The hostage hesitated, glancing back and forth from Bolan to the man-made forest with its lurking shadows, but the hostiles crouched behind the chase car finally made his mind up for him. One of them fired a shot in their direction, and the impact of his pistol round against the Lincoln's dusty flank was all it took to put the captive into lurching motion.

Bolan followed him toward the trees, swiveling to fire a single round of discouragement at the gunners. He would save the rest for any of the hunters brave enough to pursue him through the trees. He scrambled up the slope before the hardmen knew that he was gone, and found shelter in the trees.

Ahead, he heard the hostage panting, and at his back, the sounds of pursuit were shaping up. It was a race, then, with survival as the finish line, and Bolan was determined his team would finish in the money.

He overtook the other runner, pointing him in the true direction of the far perimeter. The captive was disoriented, unaccustomed to the woods at night and running for his life. It would be up to Bolan, then, to make sure that he was still alive when they came out the other side.

Assuming that they came out. No small assumption, with the pack already breathing down their necks and profiting from their familiarity with the terrain.

The soldier heard them coming, gaining, and he knew that some of them would overtake him long before he made the low retaining wall and safety. On his own, the Executioner could outdistance them with ease, employ the tactics learned in years of jungle warfare to outwit them.

But he was not alone, and Bolan's first consideration had to be the hostage, who clearly lacked the skill and stamina to win a footrace with determined hunters. And unless he meant to bring a corpse out of the forest with him, he would have to stand and fight.

Outnumbered as usual, right, but not necessarily outgunned.

He ran beside the hostage for a moment, speaking to him swiftly, making sure the other understood his orders and would follow them at least as far as the estate's perimeter.

Beyond that he would have to trust his timing, and the universe. If they were separated or if the hostage chose to strike out in some new direction...

There was no end of possible calamities, but Bolan dismissed them, clearing decks for action. Falling back, he watched for a moment as the other runner disappeared among the trees. Then the Executioner turned to face the hunters who were tracking them with murderous intent. Four guns left, and while he had faced longer odds before, the Executioner could not assume that this would be a simple kill.

He had advantages, of course: the darkness, the residue of shock from seeing others in their party killed. The hunters would be cautious, even frightened, and the Executioner could use that fear against them in the end.

They knew the land, or some of it at any rate. But crouching in the darkness and listening to their advance, Mack Bolan knew that they were more accustomed to the asphalt trails of Los Angeles, where neon turned the night to day and street signs clearly marked the territory.

More interested in speed than silence, Bolan's enemies had formed themselves into a sort of ragged skirmish line, spaced out at intervals of twenty yards. To compensate for lack of visual contact, they were calling back and forth to one another now, strained voices wafting on the night breeze, telling Bolan of their every move.

They could not have helped him more if they had painted luminescent bull's-eyes on their shirtfronts to accommodate him in the darkness.

Bolan carefully returned the AutoMag to military

leather, let the silenced Beretta 93-R take the cannon's place. A lighter weapon, it was all the gun he needed to dispose of these unwary hunters.

Bolan was a gliding shadow in the deeper gloom of the trees, maneuvering to take the gunners on their flank. He let their beckoning voices guide him home, condemning them to death.

Their flanker was heavyset, his breath the labored wheezing of a city boy unused to any sort of hiking. When he called out to the others there was something peevish, almost juvenile and pouting, in his voice, as if he wanted desperately to take his ball and quit the game.

Mack Bolan helped him out of it, the sleek Beretta sliding in to skin-touch range before he squeezed the trigger. A single parabellum mangler pinched through the target's skull, and the chunky gunner dropped without a word of protest. Bolan stepped across him, moving toward the next in line.

Number two was taller, athletic, slipping in and out among the trees as if he might have some experience with killing in nocturnal woodlands. Some, but not enough, damn straight, for Bolan took him on his blind side, wasted him with another coughing round.

Two down and two to go.

The third man was entangled in some thorny brush when Bolan found him. He was cursing underneath his breath and hacking at the branches with his pistol barrel. The Executioner helped him get the problem out of mind. Forever.

The last man was growing worried as the others failed to answer him on schedule. He was rapidly beginning to regret his eagerness in leading off the hunt, when rustling movement on his flank announced the presence of another. The gunner turned, one hand—the one without the .38— upraised in greeting for what had to be a teammate, and his voice was shaky underneath a show of irritation.

"Shit man, don't sneak up on me that way."

"Okay," Mack Bolan answered, and his second, muffled word reached out to close the gap between them, silencing the hunter's protests for eternity.

The soldier turned away from death and went to find the living, homing on the spot where he had entered the estate originally. He reached it, found himself alone and back-tracked twenty yards to either side, allowing for the darkness and a reasonable margin of error. Then he made out the huddled shape hunched against the wall and clinging to its shadow for protection.

Score one for trust, Bolan thought, and wondered just how far that trust would carry him.

The hostage flinched as Bolan suddenly emerged from the midnight shadows, but the man stood his ground until the recognition had been made.

"Is this the place?" the captive whispered.

"It's close enough," Bolan told him, reaching down to free a slim stiletto from its sheath along his calf.

Bolan felt the other man's eyes following the knife, although he did not pull away when Bolan reached for him and brought the blade in contact with his bonds. A brief stroke and he was free, massaging blood and feeling back into his hands as Bolan stowed the dagger in its sheath.

"Where do we go from here?"

"It's up and over," Bolan told him, nodding toward the stone wall at his back. "I've got a car outside."

"Not sure I'm up to it," the man replied. "I went a few rounds with the troops back there...except they did all the punching."

"No alternative," the warrior said. "I'll help you over."

And he did, pretending not to hear the hiss of pain elicited when bruised and battered flesh met rugged stone. The recent hostage spent some precious numbers balanced on the top of the wall, and when he took the plunge, his drop was graceless, obviously painful.

Bolan followed in a single fluid motion, getting there in time to help the other to his feet. He led the way along a steep defile that took them down to an unpaved access road that paralleled the canyon proper. There, beneath a drooping stand of willows, was the sportster that had brought him to the studio.

Bolan neutralized the tamperproof alarms, then stepped back to discover that the former prisoner was watching him with interest. It seemed to override the pain and fear that he had lately suffered, urging him to speak before he climbed inside the car, before he trusted Bolan any further with his life.

"Where are you taking me?" he inquired, attempting to sound casual.

Mack Bolan flashed a mirthless grin. "Away from here, for starters," he replied. "And you don't have a lot of time to think about it, Mr. Price."

The recognition had been instantaneous when Bolan had seen him huddled in the Lincoln at the ambuscade. He knew the face from television news clips and, more recently, from Johnny's photos. Some of them had shown a smiling father-daughter team, but none of them displayed the layer of steel beneath the politician's sunlamp tan.

Foster Price was frowning at him now as if by staring at the man in black he'd find the answers to the host of riddles that were plaguing him. But at the moment, Bolan had no time for questions.

"Now or never," he informed the politician. "Your choice."

Foster Price made up his mind. He brushed past Bolan, climbed into the sportster's passenger seat and closed the door behind him firmly.

Mack Bolan slid behind the wheel and fired the engine, powering along the access road without his headlights for a hundred yards or so, until they reached its intersection with State Highway 27. He knew the two-lane blacktop snaked for half a dozen miles before it reached the coast and merged with Highway 1 at Topanga Beach. If they could get that far. . .

They couldn't.

They had covered barely half a mile when Bolan spotted the scout car going south. He knew they had been seen well before the tank had swung around, its brake lights winking in the darkness. An instant later high beams were reflected in his rearview mirror as their pursuers closed the gap.

Someone inside the tank had recognized Bolan's passenger, or maybe they were checking any car encountered on the canyon road. In either case the chances of an unobstructed getaway had vanished like a fleeting shadow in the sudden glare of headlights.

The Executioner called up more speed and felt the streamlined shark respond, but on his tail the heavy Cadillac was keeping pace. There was a little something extra underneath that hood, for damn sure, and Bolan watched his final hopes for flight instead of fight evaporate.

He could still outrun them in the short stretch, Bolan knew; the sportster's better handling and lighter weight would give him an advantage on the winding mountain road. But they would still be clinging to him when he reached the coastal highway, and there was no way he intended to lead the hungry cannibals into a confrontation where civilians might be swept up in the cross fire.

That meant he had to take them in the canyon before he reached the merger point with Highway 1 and lost all hope of a killing zone devoid of innocent distractions.

He needed some combat stretch, and Bolan played a hunch to win himself the extra space. When he was twenty yards ahead with one tight curve of highway between the hare and the hounds, he quickly doused the sportster's lights and plunged the lonely stretch of canyon into dappled darkness.

The soldier knew that negotiating such a tortuous road at

speed without headlights was tantamount to suicide but it would not take him long to see if his plan would succeed or lead to lethal failure.

As he killed the lights he simultaneously slowed his charger by easing off the accelerator. They coasted for an agonizing moment, losing speed, and only when the engine seemed about to stall did Bolan shift down, running through the gears expertly and depressing the accelerator just enough to keep them moving without trying to outrun the chase car.

And his plan, if it had any chance at all, depended on the hit team overtaking them, reducing any gap to ramming range.

Behind, high beams pinned him in a spotlight like an insect nailed to a collector's mounting board. Teeth clenched, the soldier held his pace, ignoring every urge to put some ground between himself and the approaching carload of death.

At Bolan's side, the would-be senator had swiveled half around to watch the chase car, but his eyes returned at frequent intervals to search his companion's chiseled profile for some hint of what madness had compelled him to sacrifice their lead. But the granite face revealed nothing.

The warrior's rearview mirror showed the Caddy gunship almost upon them, riding up to kiss the sportster's bumper with its own, and the tank was sprouting automatic weapons from its windows.

He reached for the headlight switch and gripped it between two fingers as he counted down the final numbers. It was vital that he give them time to taste the first hot rush of victory before he snatched it back and turned it into bitter gall.

He tugged the dashboard knob and twin beams split the night ahead, illuminating tight S-turns. The maneuver had the desired effect. Behind, Bolan saw the sudden glow of his taillights reflected in the chrome of the Caddy's grille. The

crew wagon's driver obviously mistook them for the flare of
brake lights, just as Bolan hoped he would.

The big car fell back, swerved, then almost stood on its
nose. But the Executioner knew the man would be an ex-
pert. He was quick, professional, and he saved the hunting
party from complete disaster, at the same time costing them
precious seconds in the chase.

Bolan seized the opportunity and tramped on the gas,
powering away and gaining ground before the cursing
wheelman could recover from his fright and get the Caddy
back on track. The warrior took the sportster through those
S-turns, losing sight of the chase car once, twice, knowing
that another curve was all he needed.

He found it three curves farther down, a narrow gravel
turnout overhung by willows. The soldier slowed enough to
let himself maneuver, then described a tight U-turn in the
middle of the mountain roadway, reversing close into the
turnout so that they were facing back along the route of
the pursuit.

He ordered Foster Price out of the car and saw him safely
up the steep embankment behind them, concealed among
the trees. Bolan killed the sports car's engine, doused the
lights and took his place behind the open driver's door,
crouching within easy reach of steering wheel and dash con-
trols. The silver AutoMag was in his fist, the safety off and
hammer back, its cannon muzzle angled uprange to meet
the enemy when it arrived.

He did not have long to wait.

High-beam funnels appeared above him, winking
on and off as the geography afforded glimpses. The
jungle fighter waited patiently, aware that there was no
precaution he could take beyond what had been done already.

The Caddy cleared that final curve and barreled down
into the half-mile straightaway. They would be on him in
another moment, headlights picking out the sports car in

its makeshift hiding place—but Bolan did not give them time to register what they were seeing.

Reaching back inside the car, he flicked the headlights on. They had been set on High, and now the sudden glare was blinding for the Caddy's wheelman, forcing him to raise one hand and shield his eyes. Inside the chase car, Bolan saw more hands raised, some of them with weapons, but they lacked a target now.

The AutoMag roared in his fist, unloading half its magazine in rapid-fire, and Bolan watched the Caddy's windshield as it buckled, frosted over for a split second, then finally imploded. One round took the driver, punching through his upraised arm to find the face and brain concealed behind it, suddenly depriving the crew wagon of a hand upon the helm.

And the reaction was immediate, as dead weight dragged the steering wheel to one side and put the Cadillac into a smoking skid that took them past the sportster into the S-curve dead ahead...and through the flimsy guardrail posted there.

The Executioner stood in time to see the taillights winking, flashing at him as they teetered momentarily on the verge, and then the tank was gone. He followed its descent by the reverberating sounds of impact until trees below received the hurtlng weight.

He doused the lights again, returned the AutoMag to leather and was climbing back behind the wheel when Foster Price came scrambling down the slope to join him. He was dusty from the climb, his suit befouled with dirt and grass. He climbed in the passenger's side and never took his eyes off Bolan as he closed the door.

"You killed them all," he said when he could find the words. "My God."

Mack Bolan put the car in motion and proceeded in the direction of the coastal highway and Los Angeles.

"That's what I do," he told the night.

3

The motel in North Hollywood was meant to be a stopping place, nothing more. It offered none of the security of Bolan's secret Strongbase to the south, in San Diego, but it had the virtue of a desk clerk who had long ago forgotten the fine art of asking questions.

The three men were sitting around a sleazy one-room "suite," and drinking black coffee as they talked. Mack Bolan did the listening, watched Foster Price and frequently glanced at his brother, Johnny, seated on the sagging bed.

The kid had grown up well, and Bolan had good reason to be proud of him. The name was Johnny Gray now, but there was Bolan in the soul and in the strong, unbending spine.

Not much around the face, the warrior thought, and then remembered with an effort that they once looked alike, before his underground existence forced him to adopt another face, a battle mask to shield him from the hunters.

There had been other faces since those early days of Bolan's war against the Mafia, and while he underwent the changes, "the kid" was going through some changes of his own, damn right. Their paths had crossed from time to time along the hellfire trail, when Johnny sought a place beside his outlaw brother, but the Executioner had put him off. He had insisted that he go along with Val Querente's plan to marry lawyer Jack Gray, adopting Johnny in the process, changing his name and all for safety's sake.

Some changes, right, and while the Executioner was taking on the world, young Johnny Gray had made some choices of his own. He was a seasoned veteran, with a tour of duty in Lebanon behind him. He was grown and he was blooded. It had been with something close to sadness that Bolan realized there was no kid to shelter anymore.

And Johnny was aboard the team now, to a limited extent. Hell, they *were* the team, with occasional assistance from old friends on the side. Johnny kept Strongbase safe and sound, working part-time with a storefront law firm that provided him with insights into what was happening on the streets.

Insights, sure, and contacts—like the man who sat before them now, trying to make some sense of a family life that lay in ruins.

"Who knows where it starts?" the politician asked rhetorically. "My Julie was a normal kid, I guess. Rebellious sometimes, but she was never into drugs or anything like that in high school."

"As far as you know," Johnny prodded.

Foster Price nodded slowly.

"Yes. As far as I know. That's pretty sorry, huh? Well, I guess you've heard it all before. You know my job, the law firm, politics. My wife did all the work involved with raising Julie. She saw her through the little scrapes that all kids have, and when she passed away last year, well, Julie was in high school, old enough...she didn't seem to need a baby-sitter anymore. I thought she was grown up, or maybe I just didn't think at all...."

A muffled sob cut through the words, and Foster Price took a moment to compose himself. When he resumed, he sounded like a man out of condition who had just run twenty miles.

"You know the rest," he finished, glancing back and forth from Johnny Bolan to the man in black. "About tonight... I got a lead that someone back there in the can-

yon might have something on the source of Julie's...
films...her whereabouts. I had to take the chance. I just
thank God that you were there.''

"Who got in touch with you about the films originally?'' Bolan asked.

Price shrugged, his face a chiseled mask of misery.
"There were no names, just voices on the telephone, those
goddamned reels of film in plain brown wrappers. To this
day I've never heard a name or met one of the bastards
face-to-face.''

"What are they asking for?''

And Bolan knew the answer before he even asked the
question.

"Nothing much," the would-be senator replied sar-
donically. "My soul, for openers—not that I price it very
high these days. Complete allegiance to some faceless,
nameless outfit that can use an up-and-coming senator.''

"What happens if you lose?" the soldier asked.

"Ironically, there doesn't seem to be much chance of
that.'' His laugh was bitter, almost jolting in the little
room. "I'm running well ahead in all the polls right now.
Unless I die before election day, I seem to be a shoo-in.''

The man's tone told Bolan that the prospect of a preelec-
tion death had been considered seriously, but the guy was
hanging on because his daughter needed him. The soldier
gave him further points for courage, moved ahead with the
interrogation.

"What about police? The FBI? If she's been kidnapped
as you say—"

"I thought about it. I've thought of everything from
private eyes to ways I could fake an accident and get
myself disqualified because of health or..."

He left it hanging, but the specter crossed his face again,
and Bolan felt a measure of the grieving father's pain.

"I was considering the FBI again when I sat down with
Johnny, here," the candidate explained. "He talked me

into holding off until he had a look around. You know the rest."

Mack Bolan knew the rest, for sure. He had enough firsthand experience with the leeches who attempted to control the lives of others through coercion, blackmail, any dirty means at their disposal. For mafiosi and their ilk, sex was a tool, a cash commodity and, given time, they would pervert the most sublime of human actions into something that could serve their twisted purposes. Some compromising pictures of a man in public life, perhaps. And if the man himself should be too difficult to reach, then he might have a wife, a fiancée, a child. . .

He understood the anguish Foster Price was feeling from grim experience. There was no other pain quite like it in the world, and it could drive a man to desperate action if he did not keep his wits about him.

"I'm going to be honest with you," Bolan told him flatly. "We don't have a lot to go on at the moment, and we don't have any chance at all if you insist on blundering around and stirring up the other side."

"I know that I was wrong to take it on myself, but—"

"Fine." The soldier's voice prevented Price from turning it into an explanation. "If you can learn from your mistakes, I'd say your daughter has a fighting chance."

It was as close as he would come to reassurance, and he saw a mix of fear and anger on the grieving father's face.

"You think I jeopardized her, don't you?"

Bolan nodded. "Undeniably. If she had been inside that studio tonight, she might be dead right now. You *would* be dead if we had missed each other by another minute."

Price listened to his words and chose to find a ray of hope concealed behind them. "Then you think that Julie might still be alive? I mean, I had almost convinced myself that there was nothing more beside the films. . . ."

Mack Bolan shrugged, refusing to entice the man or make him any promises that might not be fulfilled.

"I won't know anything until I check it out. And what I don't need is a civilian full of good intentions getting in the way."

Or getting in the line of fire, he thought.

"But...I mean, how do you find a missing person in Los Angeles, for heaven's sake?" the politician asked.

"Ask around," the soldier told him. "And if it's necessary, there are certain cages I can rattle until something breaks."

"Like tonight."

But it was not a question.

Bolan shook his head, a firm, emphatic negative.

"Tonight was strictly by ear. I had no plans for any contact till I saw your escort. Now somebody knows you're on the scent and that you've got imported muscle."

"What you're saying is, I screwed it up," Price responded. "If they kill my daughter now, it's on my head."

Bolan knew that the man was at his limit, and he felt his brother's eyes upon him, sensed that Johnny thought he'd gone too far.

"Don't write her off too soon," he said. "She's worthless to them dead, and while you're in the running they still need a lever."

Price was staring at the hands knotted in his lap, and he did not reply. The warrior faced his brother squarely, raised an eyebrow.

"Can you safe him for a day or two? I need the stretch."

Johnny Bolan hesitated, disappointment written on his face, and it was Price who answered first.

"I can't just disappear from sight," he said. "I'm in the middle of a senatorial campaign, remember?"

"You're a target every minute you're on the street," the soldier answered coldly.

"I'll take that chance." He paused a moment, screwing up his courage, then continued. "Listen, if my daughter's valuable to them, then so am I. I mean, I am the point of this whole bloody exercise.''

The Executioner would give him that, and on consideration it appeared unlikely that the Mob would so blatantly risk a public move against the charismatic candidate with the election close at hand. They might not need him yet, but they still wanted him, and badly.

"Fair enough,'' the warrior told them both. "Go on with your campaign, and play it straight. You just picked up another aide to help you out.''

The politician glanced at Johnny and responded to the young man's almost reassuring smile with one that fell somewhere this side of feeble.

"If there is anything I can do—''

"Stay clear,'' Bolan answered. "Do exactly what they tell you and report contacts that are made. I'll work the field from my end, and with any luck we should hit on something.''

Foster Price was nodding silently, agreeing to the terms, and Bolan focused on his brother now, aware that Johnny had been watching him throughout the tension-fraught exchange.

The kid would want to fight beside him, right. Get down there in the gutter with the animals and slug it out. He had the courage, certainly, and he might even have the skills by now. But something in the Executioner refused to let him take the final step and bring his brother in as a combatant in his private war.

No matter that they both were orphaned when the guns went off in Pittsfield. Johnny was the only living link with Bolan's past, and the Executioner intended to preserve him that way.

Living, right.

The kid could do his part from inside the campaign machine as Bolan's second pair of eyes. And if the day should come that he needed a second pair of hands, then . . .

Bolan closed his mind against that day, and saw his own hands reeking with the blood of cannibals. Not yet for Johnny, no.

And if the Executioner should have his way, not ever.

4

Los Angeles had been familiar territory to the Executioner since the early days of his private war against the Mafia. Bolan had been fresh from Pittsfield when he clashed with the machine presided over by one Julian "Deej" DiGeorge, and more than anything, his conflict with the southern California Family had provided him with an appreciation of the hellfire course he had elected for himself.

Los Angeles had been an education for Mack Bolan, its lessons burned indelibly into his mind and soul.

When Deej was still in charge and running things from his palatial mansion in Beverly Hills, the family had been a festering empire of corruption.

The Executioner had beaten Julian DiGeorge, reduced his empire—temporarily—to smoking ruins. But the price was high. Bolan's Death Squad, loyal recruits committed to his cause for varied reasons of their own, was destroyed in the bloody siege, and Bolan still felt their loss despite the intervening years. He heard the silent roll call of the lost inside his head each time he thought about Los Angeles.

George Zitka had originated the idea of an elite commando squad to fight beside Mack Bolan in his long crusade, and when the talking turned to action he had lived up to the nickname "Whispering Death," which he had won in Nam. Bill Hoffower had lent the squad his demolitions expertise; Tom Loudelk his talents as a scout and infiltrator. Angelo Fontenelli and Juan Andromede had been experts in automatic weapons and light artillery, respectively, while marksmen Jim Harrington and Mark

Washington had provided backup for the Executioner's own considerable sniping skill.

The Death Squad, right. A *dead* squad in the wake of Bolan's strike against the Mafia fortress at Balboa.

And there had been other sacrificial victims for the cause. Jim Brantzen, healer, had employed his skills at plastic surgery to give the Executioner a new identity—his battle mask—before the Mob's turkey doctors used him for some hellish surgery of their own. And Robert "Genghis" Conn, the crusty old police chief of a desert hamlet, murdered in his sleep, together with his wife, because he dared defy the Mafia and shelter Bolan in the Executioner's time of need.

Ten friendly ghosts, and there were countless hostile specters out there, too, set free by Bolan's hand. But this time out he was concerned about the living. Ghosts would keep; not so the lives at stake.

Julian DiGeorge's fall had changed the scene around Los Angeles, but they were superficial changes. It was still the same old dirty game they played on those mean streets from Hollywood and Vine to Watts, in boardrooms and country clubs where moneyed men of little principle convened to plot their next foray against society. The names and faces might have changed, but there was still a Mafia out there, damned right, alive and well and living in Los Angeles.

The police had done their utmost, with a few exceptions, to contain the plague, but they could not hope to stem the tide while lawyers, legislators and the very courts they served arrayed against them. Forced to play under rules that always seemed to favor the opposing team, the cops were literally drowning in a red-tape sea.

Bolan understood the problem well, but it did not affect the conduct of his private war. In combat he would always be the one-man court of last resort. While he might on rare occasions grant reprieves to useful members of the opposition, there was no damned way on earth to cop a plea or bargain down a sentence from the Executioner.

And yet, the warrior did not see himself in vigilante terms. He did not try to legislate morality, enforce his own beliefs and values on the populace at large. He was a soldier, plain if not-so-simple, and he lived by soldier's rules. In war you killed the enemy before he did the same to you or those you cared for, right. You did not kill him for philosophy or ideology, but rather from the need to stop him dead, right now, before he did more damage to another living soul.

Bolan's enemies had condemned themselves by word and deed before the Executioner had ever crossed their twisted paths. His foes were malignant lesions eating at the soft flesh of a civilized society, and Bolan was the cauterizing agent carrying the cleansing flame to burn away their taint wherever it might be exposed. As he confided to his journal in the early stages of that endless private war, "I am not their judge. I am their judgment."

And for the second time in living memory, Los Angeles was facing judgment day.

The city's current *capo* was one Vincent Andriola, who had started as a soldier under Deej and moved up through the ranks as Bolan's war and federal prosecutions took their toll. He owed his present status more to sheer attrition than to any other factor, but he had the power, coupled with the killer instinct, which made him every bit as dangerous as Julian DiGeorge had once been in his prime. And Andriola was capable of laying down the groundwork for the blackmail scheme involving Foster Price. But then again...

The porno scene in southern California was chaotic, like some spastic Hydra with its many heads thrashing out in individual directions. Andriola's Family ran the major distribution outlets, granted, and they sometimes filmed the heavy trash themselves at places like the big Topanga studio, but there were countless other sources for the celluloid erotica that flowed out of the southland in a steady stream.

And Mack Bolan still had no leads on the source of Julie Price's films.

The visit to Topanga might have filled him in to some extent, but there could be no going back there now. The Executioner would have to find his answer elsewhere. On the street, perhaps.

He briefly cursed the fate that had led his path to cross with that of Foster Price so early in the mission. But he dismissed the train of thought and focused his concentration on the problem of the moment. It was blackmail, right, damned near the oldest game in town and one that Bolan was accustomed to from long experience. The Mafia had played this hand before in other high-stakes deals, and he remembered Washington, Saint Louis and other kill zones as if the cards had been dealt yesterday.

But this time out there was a brand-new twist. The Mob was fishing for a senator, and through his errant daughter they had hooked the brightest hopeful in a field of mostly drab contenders. With Price in hand, if they succeeded, Andriola and his mafiosi could emasculate the politician's war on crime for starters, and go on from there to wield him as a puppet in the halls of Congress.

If they succeeded.

But the Executioner had pledged to see that they did not succeed. He meant to see them die before he saw them win...and for that, he needed Julie Price.

The streets of Hollywood were calling, and he was answering. Armed with grim determination and a pocketful of photographs depicting other "stars" who shared the seedy spotlight in her films, the warrior meant to locate Julie Price if she was in Los Angeles.

If she had not been moved—by Andriola or whomever— for safekeeping when the blackmail plot was hatched.

If she was still alive.

If.

The Executioner would find her regardless of the cages that he had to shake along the way. Regardless of the heads that rolled while he was on the hunt.

Two lives were hanging in the balance, teetering between salvation and destruction while Mack Bolan held the balance weight. One step too far and he could damn them both to living hell; one step too few and he might miss his chance completely.

And everything came down to choices. The life-or-death decisions that a soldier learned to make routinely in the hellgrounds, trusting his instincts, his ability, his weapons to support the choices that he made.

It would be life-and-death again in Los Angeles, and Bolan offered up a silent prayer for guidance to the universe before he hit the streets.

The Executioner was casting players for the splatter movie of all time, and there would be no doubles, no damned stunt men listed when the final credits rolled. He was about to give "the town illusion built" a taste of bloody realism, and he hoped that everyone was hungry.

5

The streets surrendered a name and finally, a working address. The hunter parked his rental car upwind, deciding to walk. He noted that there seemed to be no continuity among the people he encountered in this neighborhood of sleazy bars and businesses. Along the short block's walk he met a human of every race and gender.

Men in stylish business suits looked sheepish or defensive as they caught his eye; the punks, decked out in leather with their spiky hair dyed every color of the rainbow, tended toward defiance seasoned with a dash of apathy. A macho body-builder type paraded past him, hand in hand with his diminutive, bearded lover.

Across the street a stoned guitarist played for the amusement of some black youths dressed in street-gang colors, and a wino occupied the vacant doorway next to his objective, grumbling fitfully in alcoholic slumber.

The target was a combination bookstore and adult arcade. It catered to the widest range of human sexual fantasies, and from quick perusal of the magazines on bold display, Mack Bolan saw that sexual encounters were not limited to humans, either. Display racks all along one wall were filled with bondage paraphernalia and an endless stock of kinky toys that bore the label Marital Aids. But Bolan's target was beyond a curtained entrance leading off the sex shop proper.

Stopping by the cashier's cage, he bought a dozen metal tokens at five dollars each, ignored the clerk's all-knowing wink and moved on toward the back. He brushed the faded curtain aside and entered a narrow, dingy corridor. Along each side were ranks of video machines that played five-minute sex shows for a dollar, but the warrior passed them by, intent upon his goal. He found it at the far end of the passageway.

Four booths the size of smallish service-station rest rooms had been built into the walls, two on either side. Directly to his front, the corridor ended abruptly at a door secured with an alarm that would alert the combination clerk and bouncer when it opened. Bolan chose the first booth on his left and pushed aside the omnipresent faded curtain, fighting down a sudden need to wash his hands.

Inside the stall a single folding chair was bolted to the floor, possibly to keep some wretch from taking off with it for parts unknown. The perfect starter for any young man furnishing a skid row pad, hell, yes. The soldier stood, reluctant to sit down where countless sweating bodies must have hunched and strained in passion's grip. Their memory was thick upon the air already, almost nauseating in its strength.

He thumbed a token into a slot set against one wall, and a kind of giant shutter levitated out of sight, revealing that the wall in front of him was made of thick plate glass.

Beyond the pane a tall black woman stood with legs apart and hands on hips, wearing only a slender golden chain around her waist. A spotlight set into the ceiling illuminated every inch of her, and she seemed to be basking in the glow. She had a chair like Bolan's in her little cubicle, except that hers had not been bolted to the floor, and now she moved it closer to the window, planting one leg on the seat, her pelvis angled toward him.

One hand slid along her abdomen, brightly painted nails circling her pubic area. She snared a wall-mounted telephone receiver and nodded toward its counterpart on Bolan's side.

He raised the handset gingerly with thumb and forefinger, held it short of contact with his flesh. The woman's breathing singed his ear.

"It's your time, babe," she said. "Just tell me what you want."

He told her.

"Cherry Gifford."

Teasing fingers ceased their restless dance and surprise was vying with suspicion in her eyes. Suspicion won.

"Who are you, man?"

He palmed a hundred-dollar bill and held it up against the glass.

"I need to find her. Is she working?"

"Maybe."

The bill was halfway to his pocket when she stopped him.

"Hey, okay, she's working, man. Her stall's across the way, there."

Bolan frowned.

"You wouldn't shuck me, would you?"

"No way." There was an earnestness that spoke of hunger in her voice. "She's over there. You check it out."

"She'd better be."

The tone informed her that she would not like the consequences if he came back disappointed.

"Honest, man, she's there. No shit."

Bolan replaced the receiver on its hook and slid the bill through a little mail-drop slot that had been cut into the glass for customers inclined toward tipping. Then he scrambled out of there, moving across the hall and through another curtained entrance.

Another token in the slot, and this time when the shutter rose the soldier had his mark.

She was a slim Caucasian, full of breast despite her size and youth, with tawny hair that framed a street-wise angel face, and Bolan recognized that face without resorting to the photograph he carried. She was as naked as her counterpart across the hall, and from the pose she struck, complete with lifted leg and searching hand, he guessed the working girls relied on rehearsed routines.

"What would you like?"

"I need some information, Cherry."

Just a flicker of surprise behind the jade-green eyes, and she was on her guard as she dropped the raised leg and faced him squarely.

"How'd you know my name? Are you the heat?"

"I'm private," Bolan told her. "And we've got a friend in common. One I'd like to find."

"Oh, yeah? Who's that?"

He saw the risk and took his chances.

"Her name is Julie Price, but she may not have used it lately."

"Sure. I know how that goes."

There was still suspicion in her face, her posture, but the news that he was not police had loosened her a little. She was working ang'es now inside her head, and he could almost hear the wheels in motion as he searched for an advantage in the game of one-on-one they were playing.

Bolan raised a photo of his quarry to the glass and held it there for her inspection. Cherry Gifford hesitated, chewing on her lower lip, and Bolan thought she should have been in school somewhere fretting over math instead of standing naked underneath a spotlight, scanning mug shots.

"Yeah, I recognize her," Cherry said at last. "And she was Julie, except I'm not too sure about the last name."

Fair enough. It was a start, at any rate.

"When was the last time you saw her?"

"Hey, man, this ain't twenty questions," she responded petulantly. "We get didley shit around this place without the tips we make from customers, you know? You're taking up my time."

The Executioner held up a thousand-dollar bill this

time—the kind they do not put in circulation anymore—
and let her feast her eyes upon the string of zeros for a moment.

"A grand? Well, hey, now...if she's into something
heavy..."

"That's the word," he told her. "But her trouble's not
with me. I'm trying to pull her clear."

The woman behind the glass was searching Bolan's face
for something in the way of confirmation, and apparently
she found it, though some doubts remained.

"Well, anyway...I know you're not a cop," she said at
last as if it answered everything. "If I knew something that
could help you..."

Bolan wagged the G-note at her silently. It made the difference.

"What the hell. Why not? I'll be off work at four."

He checked his watch. Two hours.

"No go," he told her. "I don't have the time."

She frowned.

"Hey, listen, man...this job may look like shit, but
right now it's all I've got." She hesitated, finally surrendered to the urge for explanations. "I'm an actress,
like, you know? Except that parts are kinda hard to find
right now."

Without a word he tore the bill in two and slid one portion of it through the mail drop in the window, feeling her
astonished eyes upon him as he straightened again.

"You get the other half and four more like it when we're
finished," he informed her. "If we leave right now."

And this time Cherry Gifford did not hesitate.

"You've got yourself a deal. I'll need a coupla minutes
to get ready."

"Fine."

The shutter fell between them, cutting off the soldier's
view of wistful green eyes. He cursed the fates or the
society—whatever—that had driven such a human being to

seek her meager fortunes in the street among the jackals, and he put that reeking cubicle behind him.

Bolan killed five minutes at the magazines, pretending now and then to read one. But his mind was not in focus on the snapshots showing everything from bestiality to bondage in excruciating detail. He was looking toward the future, trying to anticipate the pitfalls that the coming hours held, but it was hopeless, and he gave it up before he felt the woman's presence at his elbow.

"Ready," she announced, and looking at her, Bolan had no choice but to agree.

She wore a pair of tight, hip-hugging jeans, with legs tucked into knee-high boots. Somehow, the simple outfit made her even more alluring than when she was displayed in total nudity beyond the window of the peep-show cubicle.

And there was something to be said for mystery, damn right, in women as in warfare.

The woman-child was one exciting animal, but their lives were out of sync, and this was not the time, the place for any urges short of raw survival.

"Ready," he confirmed, and they were moving toward the exit when a sharp voice hailed them from the cashier's cage.

"Hey, where the hell you think you're going, Cherry?" it demanded.

"Out," she answered, never breaking stride.

"Fuck that." The voice was closer now and gaining fast. "You've got a shift to finish, goddammit."

Cherry Gifford halted, turned to face the human weasel who had sold the Executioner his tokens.

"Screw my shift, Balducci. Screw this dump...and screw you, too."

"I haven't got the time, and you haven't either," the weasel cracked. There was cautious fire behind his eyes as he addressed himself to Bolan. "I don't know what kinda deal you made, Slick, but it'll have to wait until she gets off work, okay?''

The rodent reached for Cherry's arm but never found it. Bolan interposed himself between them with a single cat-like motion, fending off the outstretched hand. The color in the man's cheeks was anger now as he assessed the opposition.

"Well, if you want her that bad—"

And he rushed, a move both ill-conceived and poorly executed. Bolan fired a looping right that splayed the rodent nose across his face. A vicious left hook followed, and Bolan put his heart into it, calling up the deep reserves of fury from his soul. Explosive impact drove the bouncer backward, almost airborne as he hit the plate-glass fronting on a giant showcase. He plunged through it with a strangled little scream. They left him there, stretched out among the scattered sex toys, as they exited the shop together.

And outside, the night was waiting.

6

"You said you were an actress."

"Yeah, well, from those snaps you're carrying around, I guess you've seen some samples of my work."

She waited for him to condemn her, and when he never got around to it, the lady started to relax a little.

"I guess you've heard the stories, right? About the dumb-ass kids who come out here expecting streets of gold and wind up in the gutter for their trouble? Well, it's true for some, I guess, but me...I sort of started in the gutter and just stayed there."

Bolan did not buy that for an instant, and he told her so. The jade-green eyes were almost grateful as they watched his profile.

"Everybody's got their burdens, Cherry. Is that your real name?"

Laughter, soft but strained through bitterness. "You've got to promise you won't laugh if I tell you."

Bolan promised.

"It's Belinda. But the Gifford's real."

"Belinda," he repeated. "Nothing there to laugh at."

"It's country," she protested. "Country wasn't selling when I came out. Maybe now...I don't know. Anyway, I'm Cherry. That's pretty funny, right?"

Bolan did not find a damned thing funny in the lady's pain.

She brought back painful memories, the kind that surfaced at the damnedest times. Memories of Cindy, Bolan's younger sister, cornered by the Mafia and forced into a life of prostitution to protect her father from the loan sharks who held notes against his soul. The only sister, gone now, all her years of promise swept away when tragedy descended on the Bolan household, leaving carnage in its wake.

It was a miracle, the soldier knew, that Johnny Bolan had survived.

A miracle. . . or destiny?

"How did you get your start out here?" he asked, already knowing several versions of the answer. But each story varied slightly from the last, and if there might be any clue to help him track down Julie Price, the Executioner would have to go for it.

"You mean 'What's a nice girl like me. . . ?' "

He nodded, feeling color in his cheeks.

"No need to talk about it," he allowed. "I bought your services as guide, not your biography."

"That's really all you want from me? I mean, five grand—"

"That's all," he said. "It's worth the five if you can take me where I need to go."

"Keep driving."

They continued on in silence for a few more moments, driving east on Sunset, watching as the neon night slid past the rental car. When Cherry Gifford spoke again her voice was softer, with a hint of introspection.

"I always liked the movies," she said, and her wistful smile was reflected in the window to her right. "It looks like anyone could do it, right? I mean, just get up there, be yourself and let the good times roll."

Another silence, and the warrior sensed that it had been some time since any good times had rolled around for Cherry Gifford.

"I was seven when my old man split," she said, surprising Bolan with her change in tack. "He couldn't take it anymore, the way my mother used to cat around, and one day he just left. I guess he had no use for me. Like mother, like daughter, right?''

"Not necessarily."

"You say. But try it on the other end."

She took a moment to collect her thoughts again before resuming.

"After daddy took off my mother had a field day. I think she must've been just waiting for him to leave. Anyway, I had about a dozen fathers in the next eight years or so, and some of them began to notice I was growing up, you know?''

He knew, and hated knowing.

"I tried to tell my mother once, but she just said that I was jealous of the greasy bastard she was living with. She belted me around some, told me that I'd better never spread those kind of filthy lies again."

She hesitated, tried to swallow all the hurt in her voice, and did not quite succeed.

"It just got worse from there on out. One night, this prince of hers brings home a couple of his friends. . . . ''

He waited out the silence as she watched another block slip past, reliving private horrors inside herself.

"I split, that's all," she said at length. "And here I am."

"How long?" he asked her.

"Going on three years."

That made her old enough to vote, just barely, and in one short lifetime she had witnessed more hell on earth than many people saw by middle age. The warrior's heart went out to her, but there was nothing he could do about the past.

Together, there just might be something they could do about the future.

"What about yourself?" she asked him. "Here I am spilling things I haven't thought about in years, and I don't even know your name."

"LaMancha," Bolan told her, falling back upon a combat alias that he had used in other Mafia campaigns. "It's Frank, to you."

"So, Frank, what's the story?"

Bolan kept it clean and simple.

"Julie Price has family looking for her. All they want is safe return."

The woman-child was watching him, one eyebrow raised. "They know she's in the life?"

The warrior nodded.

"And they still want her back?" She sounded as if nothing could be more unnatural.

Another nod.

"So, when you find this Julie, *if* you find her..."

"Then I take her home," he finished for her. "Plain and simple."

And there was no reason to inform Cherry that in all probability it would be neither plain nor simple in the doing.

"Maybe she'll just run away again, you know?"

"Maybe. Anyway, she'll have the choice. Look, if you know where to find her..." he began.

"Well, not exactly."

Bolan's sudden gaze pinned her to the seat, and she hastened to explain.

"Like, there's this guy called Zoot. I think his last name's Mitchell, something like that. Anyway, he does some casting for the flickers."

"Go on."

"He cast me for a coupla flicks I worked in with this Julie that you're looking for. I figure he may have a line on where she is and what she's into lately."

It was sounding pretty thin, and Bolan told her so.

"You don't know Zoot," she countered simply. "Once he has a line on you, it's good for life."

And Bolan knew the type, of course. The leeches who

would prey upon the fears and insecurities of a struggling actress, channeling them into the sleazy world of porno films and prostitution. Male or female, it made no difference. Not precisely pimps, his type were body brokers, delivering their pound of flesh, for a price.

The clients on the vulture's line were his for life, as long as he could use them—in the films that he promoted or through outright sale to some procurer's working stable. Sometimes when the pigeon managed to escape to another life aboveground, there would be the possibility of blackmail through the threatened revelation of a sordid past.

It was another step along the trail at any rate, and Bolan could not afford to pass it up. He hoped that he could trust Belinda Gifford, knowing that his life was on the line if she should fail him.

And he did not care to think about what he must do if she turned out to be not guide, but Judas goat.

"Where do we find this Zoot?" he asked her simply, keeping all emotion from his voice.

She half turned in the bucket seat to face him, features lost in shadow from the glaring backlight as she answered.

"He's at Hotel Hell."

7

By official estimates there are between three thousand and four thousand runaways in Hollywood at any given moment. They are the "street kids": homeless, largely destitute, some preying on the public, others preyed upon in turn by human jackals. Cut off by choice or circumstance from families and friends, the vagrants band together on the street or seek a solitary life among the shadows, falling back on drugs of every sort to mask the pain that is their daily bread.

In the whole of L.A. County there are forty-one "official" beds provided for the children of the streets by public agencies, another twenty by assorted private groups throughout the sprawling county. So, assuming only Hollywood is counted, there is one safe bed for every eighty homeless kids—a frightening portrait of the new society.

Another source of refuge are crash pads; a natural response by homeless youths to their survival instincts. Some are abandoned buildings, others small motels or second-rate apartments where the kids can pool their meager earnings for the rent. Still others sleep beneath the countless freeway bridges, in abandoned cars or in the city parks.

And some wind up in Hotel Hell.

Condemned since 1980, legally off limits and surrounded by a sagging chain-link fence, the Garden Court Apartments showed their age. Graffiti artists had transformed the dingy outer walls into a psychedelic billboard.

Life was cheap inside the hollow rooms and hallways of the one-time luxury development, and it had already entered street mythology as the most dangerous of the two-dozen crash pads serving Hollywood's lost generation.

The Executioner drove slowly down Las Palmas, taking in the garish sights and sounds that were a staple of the neighborhood, his mind at work on battlefield logistics. Despite the hour, there were scores of people on the street, some occupying curbs, scanning motorists with hungry hookers' eyes, the rest drifting aimlessly along the sidewalks. If he had been in search of drugs he could have stopped and bagged his limit anywhere on the street as trading flourished in plain sight. Outlandish costumes, hollow eyes and burned-out faces made him wonder just how many of the children had already overshot their tolerance and taken one irrevocable step beyond reality.

He cleared his mind and focused on his problem in the here and now.

Correction. *Problems.*

First there was the girl, an unknown quantity in Bolan's volatile equation. She seemed sincere, but Bolan knew he could not count on her for any help if he ran into trouble on this unfamiliar ground. If it came down to killing, on the streets or in the crowded corridors of Hotel Hell, she would be nothing but an added weight around his neck.

His second problem was the hunting ground itself.

Bolan had always opted for an open field of fire if he could find it. Overall, he sought to screen innocents from the line of fire whenever he engaged the enemy. But this time, on the busy streets of Hollywood, there were no open fields of fire, no routes of flight from Hotel Hell that would not place the drifting passersby at risk.

So be it, then.

He made a slow full circle of the Garden Court Apartments and the block surrounding, taking in the neighborhood, the sagging chain-link fence with countless openings where transient residents of Hotel Hell came in and out at will. He half expected to discover squad cars parked on every corner, but surprisingly, the open sewer seemed to draw no real attention from police.

"This place get staked out much?" he asked the girl.

"No more. They used to hassle everybody on the street, you know? But now there's just so many that the cops sit back and wait for something to come in. A killing, something like that, okay?"

Bolan found a narrow alley that appeared to be unoccupied and parked the rental car beneath the shadow of a dying elm tree. Exiting, he spent a moment checking his hardware, then locked up.

Side by side, they hiked the half block back to reach a ragged opening in the chain-link fence. Bolan pushed the wire aside for Cherry and followed her into the grounds of the Garden Court Apartments.

A short walk and they were on a wide front porch with access to the rooms inside through massive double doors. A pair of scraggly punks with rainbow hair and greasy, faded denims stood near the entrance. Both came to life as Bolan and the girl approached, the youth on the left halfheartedly attempting to conceal the joint he was smoking, finally giving up the effort as he seemed to recognize the girl.

"Hey, Cherry? What it is?"

"Hey, Pink."

Bolan fought an urge to laugh. Both youths were eyeing him suspiciously, examining for telltale signs that might betray him as a narc.

"Say, Cherry, who's the citizen?" the one called Pink inquired.

"He's my new old man," she said.

A puzzled frown as Pink attempted to assimilate the information.

"Hey. That's solid."

Bolan took it for approval and followed Cherry past the two young men and through the double doors.

The odor of the place was staggering. There was a certain mustiness coupled with reeking scents of life in hiding: unwashed bodies, urine, feces, vomit, ancient marijuana smoke, loveless sex—and something else, which Bolan finally picked out and identified from all the other scents.

The smell of fear.

And Bolan knew that the denizens of Hotel Hell and places like it throughout Hollywood were under siege. From the police, social workers, hungry street gangs and the savage loners who cohabited their seamy universe. They might be cheated, raped, abused, even murdered, without meaningful recourse to the established system. And when that grim message finally made its lasting mark upon the soul, then they in turn went savage, striking out against society in some demented fantasy of self-defense.

There was no law in Hotel Hell except survival of the fittest, and Mack Bolan knew that law by heart. He had been living by it all his life, damn right, and now, despite the unknown odds against him, grim experience was on the jungle fighter's side.

They moved along a dingy corridor on threadbare carpet until they reached a staircase leading to the floors above.

"No elevators," Cherry told him simply. "Sorry."

Bolan did not mind the stairs, in fact. They made for slow retreats in time of need, but they also afforded him a chance to watch for any ambush laid along their track.

They climbed two flights and passed a single stoned-out straggler, brushing past him without seeming to disturb his private reverie.

On the third-floor landing, Cherry led him off along another hallway. Halfway down she paused outside an open door that emitted candlelight into the blacked-out corridor. She hesitated, listening at the door, and Bolan waited for her, picking up the sound of male voices from inside.

One sounded frightened, trapped, and he was catching hell from the other.

"Goddammit," number one was raging, "when I send you out to do a job, I want it fucking done, you understand?"

"I hear you, Zoot."

"So what's the problem, man? Eh? You homesick now, you little jerk?"

"No way, Zoot. I ain't going back there, ever."

"I oughta stick your sorry ass back on that Greyhound bus tonight. Right now."

"No. Please."

" 'No, please,' " the other mocked him cruelly, taunting. "You're no frigging good to me around here if you won't do what I tell you."

Sobbing now, as number two broke down.

"I'm sorry, Zoot. I swear, I won't screw up again."

"You damn sure won't."

A fleshy sound of impact followed by a bleat of pain, and Bolan shouldered past the woman-child on through the open doorway. In the candlelight a slender, dark-haired man was grappling with a youth approximately half his size. His fist was cocked to launch another blow, but Bolan stopped him with a word.

"Enough."

A violent shove propelled the boy halfway across the room, then the dark man turned to face Bolan.

"Yeah? Says who?"

His eyes were scouring Bolan in the flickering light, alert for any sign of law-enforcement hardware on his person, finding nothing that would mark him as the heat. He did not wait for Bolan's answer.

"This place is mine," he said. "You got yourself a warrant, man?"

The Executioner advanced another step into the room.

"No warrants, Zoot. This little visit's strictly unofficial."

"Well, you can haul your unofficial ass right out of here the way you came in, Clyde. I don't give interviews."

Mack Bolan closed the gap between them with a speed that took his adversary by complete surprise. He snared a handful of the human reptile's shirtfront, lifting him until his toes were almost out of contact with the floor.

"You make a poor host," he growled.

The guy was making strangled little noises, wheezing as Bolan's knuckles pressed against his windpipe, but it was another sound that warned the Executioner of danger on his flank.

The scrape of boot heels over floorboards, right, and sounds of breathless, desperate struggle close at hand.

He turned and took Zoot with him, airborne, as he faced the open doorway leading to the hall outside. Two hulking figures occupied the foreground now, one of them holding Cherry crushed against his chest, a meaty hand across her mouth to stifle any warning sound. The other stood to one side, and his fist was wrapped around the longest switch-blade the Executioner had ever seen.

"You got a problem, Zoot?" the blademan asked.

Zoot nodded jerkily, and then addressed himself to Bolan from on high.

"Hey, man," he rasped, "I don't believe you've met my welcoming committee."

8

Bolan hesitated for a heartbeat before he made his move. That blade was the immediate threat, but he was concentrating on the thug who had one meaty arm around the lady's neck. No weapon yet in evidence, but he could still do lethal damage with a sudden twist before the Executioner could reach him after dealing with the first goon.

Precision timing was required to pull it off.

The soldier moved, investing every ounce of strength and anger into a shove that propelled Zoot backward, his feet still off the floor. The human cannonball collided with a wall, the breath slammed out of him before he folded, gasping, to the floor.

Then Bolan pivoted to face the welcoming committee, his posture giving no hint of the tension he felt. He could have shot them both while their eyes were on their fallen leader, but rejected it as too risky for the woman.

"You boys got something on your mind?" he asked sarcastically. "Or did you come to see your buddy get his ass kicked?"

"You're messin' with my man," the blademan snarled, a chopping motion of his switchblade indicating Zoot.

"I'll make a mess of you," the soldier told him mockingly, advancing several cautious paces.

The knifeman rushed Bolan then, bellowing an incoherent cry of fury as he closed the gap. Bolan stood his ground until the final instant, fading left before the foot-long blade could pierce his vitals. He reached out with both hands to seize the sweaty wrist.

He went in low beneath the rush and used the punk's own weight to complete the classic movement. Blademan never knew that he was flying until meaty shoulders met the floor with crushing force.

Bolan followed through the move, applying pressure to the wrist until it snapped and lifeless fingers gave up purchase on the knife. Without emotion, Bolan drove a crushing heel against the street thug's windpipe, taking out a section of his jawbone in the process. Final spasms, tremors passing into nothingness, and he was still at last.

One to go. The one with Cherry, right.

Somewhere behind him, the scum Zoot was moving sluggishly, still fighting for a decent breath, and Bolan put him out of mind again. No danger there.

It was a calculated risk, but the warrior decided to try for fear. He slid a hand inside his jacket, came out with the sleek Beretta 93-R, its silent muzzle angling in the direction of the woman and her captor.

"Hey, man, don't get no weird ideas, because I'll take her off, you know? I mean, you can't shoot me without you hit her, too."

"Could be," the soldier told him coolly. "On the other hand, this magazine holds fifteen rounds, so even if I miss your fat ass fourteen times..."

He left it hanging, and his adversary got the message, disbelief registering across his grimy face.

"You wouldn't waste her, man. I don't believe it."

Bolan took a moment lining up the shot. "So, suit yourself," he told number two. "Your boyfriend didn't think I could take his shiv away and smash his throat, either."

That did it for the punk. He thrust Cherry Gifford hard away from him and sprinted for the open doorway. Bolan spent a moment considering alternatives: the risk of this one bringing reinforcements stacked against the odds that he would just keep running until he found a hole to hide in.

The odds and fleeting mercy made the choice. He eased

his finger off the trigger, watching as his target disappeared around the corner of the corridor. Then the soldier turned his full attention back to those around him in the dingy room.

The woman first.

"Are you okay?"

She nodded, one hand up and rubbing her neck where redness showed from chafing contact. Her voice was shaky when she spoke.

"I'm fine, yeah." Now her eyes were on the prostrate hoodlum, limp, unmoving. "Is he..."

"Dead," the warrior said.

He flicked a glance in the direction of the boy who had been catching hell from Zoot. The youth was huddling in a shadowed corner, trying hard to make himself invisible. Bolan put him out of mind and turned back to the original objective, mercy banished from his face and manner as he closed upon the human target.

Zoot was struggling to rise, still having trouble breathing when the soldier reached him. Stretching out one hand, Bolan seized a fistful of the hoodlum's greasy hair and jerked him upright, almost on his tiptoes. Wide eyes were level with his own, despite the street punk's smaller size.

"We were about to have some words when we were interrupted," he reminded Zoot unnecessarily.

"I don't know anything," the rodent said, gasping.

"Ordinarily, I might agree with you on that. But this time," Bolan said, "I think you may have just the information I need."

"Like what?"

A cautious feeler, probing for some way out of the nightmare that had cornered him and held him hostage.

"I'm looking for a flick producer," Bolan told him. "Your kind."

Sudden hope behind the rodent eyes.

"Hey... there's a lot of 'em around, you know? Just let

me have a name, and I'll arrange an introduction for you.''

Bolan's fingers tightened, twisting at the oily hair.

''I wouldn't be here if I had the name, now would I, Zoot?''

''I can't name all the skin-flick artists in L.A. We'd be here for a friggin' month.''

''I only need one name,'' Grim Death informed him.

''Yeah, I dig it, man. But how am I supposed to know—''

Bolan's free hand slid inside his coat and came out holding Julie Price's photograph. He lifted it until it was eye level with the punk.

''You know this face.'' It was not a question. ''All I want is one name and you can walk away from this.''

''That's great, man...only let's say someone else don't share your feelings?''

''One step at a time,'' the warrior told him. ''You've still got to live past me before they get a shot at you.''

''Bum odds,'' Zoot said dejectedly. ''This guy you're looking for gets off on paybacks, dig it? I start to throw his name around, I'm dead.''

Bolan put the snapshot back inside his coat and drew the 93-R once again. He let the muzzle come to rest beneath a bloodshot eye.

''So take your pick,'' he said without emotion.

The desperate eyes reached out for Cherry Gifford, pleading, and the rodent lips were taking shape around a word when Bolan ground the autoloader's snout deeper into cheek flesh.

''Make it something I want to hear,'' he cautioned.

''The Iceman,'' Zoot blurted suddenly. ''That's the only name I have on 'im.''

''How do you reach him?'' Bolan prodded.

Rasping laughter, sharp, almost hysterical.

''He reaches me,'' the hoodlum countered. ''When he needs merchandise, I get a call. I haven't even got a number for the guy, I swear.''

"How does he take delivery?" Bolan asked. "You must get paid somehow."

"Well, naturally...I mean...he picks someplace like a motel, you know, or sometimes it's an office, like. I send somebody over with the goods and they bring home the bread."

"Where would I start if I was looking for an Iceman?" Bolan asked.

Zoot's grin was vacant, disbelieving.

"Inside the freezer, man, like at the morgue. This dude is cold, you follow? You don't wanna find him."

Bolan searched the nervous eyes, decided that the other man was leveling. Reluctantly, he let go of the tangled hair and watched Zoot slump back to the floor.

"White flag," the jungle fighter said, stowing the pistol in its shoulder harness. "One time only. If I find out you've been lying to me..."

"It's straight, man, never fear."

"I'm not, Zoot. You should be."

Bolan headed for the exit, Cherry falling into step beside him. At the doorway Bolan paused and glanced back at the young man standing in the shadows, confusion written on his face.

"You coming?" Bolan asked him simply.

Hesitation, and a jerky nod of affirmation.

"Yeah, I guess."

"Hey, man—"

Zoot never had a chance to finish as the warrior pinned him with a steely glare.

"Let's go," Bolan growled.

The youth trailed them back along the murky corridor toward the staircase. Bolan led the way as they descended, and they were halfway to the second landing when a looming shadow barred their path.

The second half of Zoot's late welcoming committee, sure.

Bolan breathed a silent curse. So much for the odds, god-dammit. And so much for mercy, right.

He made a rapid head count, quitting when he got to nine and knowing there were more around the corner, waiting out of sight. The pointman had two barrel-chested bikers on his flank, chains and Nazi badges dangling from their greasy vests, one of them decked out in a World War II German helmet. Behind the front rank, punks with spiky, multicolored hair and war paint on their faces brandished boards and lengths of pipe.

"He's got a piece," the one-man welcoming committee told his flankers. "Watch his hands."

"I don't care if he's got a fuckin' M-16," the biker with the helmet snarled, unraveling a length of chain that he wore looped around his waist. "I'm gonna waste his ass."

Above Bolan, Cherry and the younger man had started their retreat in the direction of the third-floor landing, but another figure blocked their path.

"This guy's the heat!" Zoot shouted down at the assembled troops. "He's gonna shut us down around here if you let 'im."

Angry rumbling, then a tidal surging in the ranks. Mack Bolan stood his ground, still made no move to reach the autoloader slung beneath his arm.

"Well, what's it going to be?" he asked the leader of the pack. "You want it one-on-one, or do you like banana style?"

"Hey, what the—"

"You know," he told the simian pointman, speaking loudly to include them all. "That's everyone together in a yellow bunch."

The rumbling became a roar of outrage, and they came for him.

Banana style.

9

The lead man was on top of Bolan when the 93-R cleared leather. He leveled it and triggered off a single shot at point-blank range. The parabellum shocker drilled his target underneath one eye and blew a fist-sized exit hatch in back, distributing the contents of his skull among the rear-guard troops. They faltered back there, scrambling aside as muzzle blast and gravity propelled the pointman backward through their ranks.

The big bikers, undeterred and growling like a pair of Norse berserkers, cleared the final risers leading to their human target. Bolan swiveled, raised an arm against the falling chain and stroked another silenced round out of the autoloader.

The greasy Viking on his right stumbled, clapping one broad hand against a crimson stain that blossomed in the center of his chest.

Then a numbing pain blazed down the length of Bolan's upraised arm and he fell backward, going down beneath the weight of biker number two. Bolan twisted underneath him and brought his knees up, struggling to find some purchase that would let him throw the crushing burden off. The German helmet slammed into his face with stunning force, and he could taste the blood that filled his mouth before he found the angle he needed.

Straining, Bolan lashed out with both legs, driving his adversary back, precariously balanced on the stairs as he unlimbered the Beretta. Two quick rounds took the biker underneath his shaggy chin and lifted him completely off his feet. The almost headless body wobbled through a clumsy backward somersault and plowed into the milling reinforcements, toppling them like bowling pins.

The jungle fighter made it to his feet, already thumbing down the switch to convert the 93-R to 3-shot mode. He stroked the trigger once, sent three rounds burning through the plaster inches from the punkers' rainbow-colored scalps. They got the message and scattered down the stairwell.

He spun around to face the other enemy, but Zoot was already grappling with the youth who had attached himself to Bolan's little force. The two of them were fighting silently while the woman stood well back, pressed against one grimy wall.

As Bolan moved to intervene, Zoot drove a vicious underhand into his adversary's stomach. And like magic, the switchblade belonging to his former bodyguard materialized in Zoot's right hand, flashing toward the youngster's throat.

He never made that fatal cut, as Bolan's automatic rounds ripped through his cheek and temple. Zoot seemed to sag, wet pieces of him forming an abstract pattern on the wall where he had stood a heartbeat earlier.

Bolan reached the boy and helped him straighten. Cherry Gifford was still gaping at the carnage in the stairwell, making little sounds that told the warrior she was close to losing it. But there was no damned time to coddle her. Not while they still remained in Hotel Hell with two more hostile floors below them to negotiate.

"Will they be waiting for us?" Bolan asked.

It was the boy who answered, speaking through his pain and from his knowledge of the denizens.

"Probably. You scared 'em good, but Zoot was special, kinda father figure. Yeah, it could be hairy goin' down there when they get their nerve back."

"Okay, no choice," Bolan told them. "We're going

down. From here on out assume that every living thing's an enemy and act accordingly.''

The young man nodded and bent to grasp the knife that had been meant for him some moments earlier. He hefted it and turned it over in his smallish hands, then finally let it hang beside him, blade down, like the short sword of a young centurion prepared to face the unknown enemy.

Except that to this youth, the enemy was only too well-known. They were his people, turned against him now, and he had lived among them long enough to know their feral instincts. Bolan wondered if he would be able to confront them with the same instinctive courage he had shown in tackling Zoot. If so, the boy might have a chance of getting out of Hotel Hell alive.

The lady did not arm herself, and Bolan understood her feelings, how the killing she had witnessed in the past few moments must have shaken her. He only hoped that she retained enough raw courage and determination to see her through what they still had to do. And from what the boy had said the worst might well be yet to come.

He faced the boy and said, ''I didn't catch your name.''

''It's Heath,'' he said. ''Heath Mohawk.''

''Frank LaMancha,'' Bolan told him, coming close enough, at least in spirit, to the truth.

They shook hands, man and boy. Two men now, with, perhaps, a grisly job ahead of them.

Warrior Bolan's mind was on the numbers as they started down, he leading, Cherry Gifford in the middle for security, and young Heath Mohawk and his captured switchblade bringing up the rear.

Bolan wondered just how many drifters, bikers and the like might occupy the corridors and empty rooms of Hotel Hell.

Too many, right.

They gained the landing on the second floor and paused there, taking stock of their surroundings. Two floors above them now and one below, with fifty yards of dark, foreboding corridor between the staircase and their final exit on the street. Bolan felt as if he was a piece of meat inside a sandwich, waiting for his enemy to take that first bite.

When that bite came, he meant to break as many of the opposition's teeth as he could and ram his fury down their goddamned throats as a surprise dessert. Let them chew on death awhile and find out how they liked the flavor.

Bolan and his little makeshift team were halfway to their ground-floor destination when three shadows maneuvered into view below them, sealing off the bottom of the stairwell. Bolan did not recognize them from the skirmish fought upstairs, but they were armed identically, with lengths of chain, an ice pick and something that resembled an abbreviated pitchfork.

"Back off," Bolan warned, knowing even as he spoke that it was futile. They knew that he was armed, and they had made the choice to face him anyway, too doped-up or burned-out to give a damn.

Fine.

He raised the 93-R, finger taut around the trigger, but before he had a chance to fire, a warbling shriek from overhead pierced the confines of the dingy stairwell. Bolan swiveled toward the sound just in time to see a body plummet feetfirst toward the stretch of staircase that his little task force occupied.

The jumper, tall and as black as night, decked out in street-gang colors, touched down on the stairs a dozen feet above Bolan, landing in a crouch that left him ready for defense or offense at a second's notice. There was something in his hand—a Boy Scout hatchet—and as Bolan moved to intercept, the newcomer lunged directly at Heath Mohawk, swinging wildly, shouting like a madman.

Mohawk ducked beneath the first swing, the hatchet's head sinking into the plaster wall. The youth brought his knife up, gripped in both hands, and the blade disappeared into pliant flesh. Sheer momentum disemboweled the enemy, and Mohawk recoiled, the long knife blood-slick to its hilt as he held it in front of him to face a second charge that never came. Clutching his intestines, the black man staggered backward and sprawled onto his back, dead eyes wide open.

Downrange, Bolan's enemies rushed him, jostling one another as they tried to climb the stairs together, three abreast. He pivoted to face them, held the trigger down and let his weapon empty its magazine in automatic fire at almost point-blank range.

His targets seemed to stumble, going down together in an awkward tangle that was arms and legs and spastic death throes all rolled into one. There was no sound from any of them save the thumping of one's boot heels as he kicked out feebly against the wall.

The jungle fighter ditched his empty magazine and snapped a fresh one into the pistol grip. He worked the action swiftly, chambering a live one as the other members of his little squad moved down to join him in the no-man's-land between fresh corpses.

"Homestretch," he told them. "Are you ready?"

"Ready," Mohawk echoed, something between excitement and determination etched into the young-old face.

A silent nod from Cherry Gifford, but Bolan noted that she was armed now. The late high-flier's hatchet seemed incongruous in slender hands with brightly painted nails.

Incongruous and deadly—if she had the nerve to use it when the chips were down.

They reached the ground floor, entering the final darkened corridor in single file. The soldier switched his side arm back to semiauto mode, preferring accuracy and selective conservation of his last two magazines above wild automatic firing in the dark, where every shadow seemed to be a lurking enemy.

Darting shapes moved across his field of vision at the far end of the hall, and he resisted the temptation to take pot-shots at them. Time enough for that if they were cornered.

A door banged open almost in his face and toppled off its one remaining hinge to partly block the corridor as two figures sprang into his path. Some sort of heavy weapon—ax or shovel, Bolan did not have the time to know or care—sliced air above his head, almost decapitating him but for his lightning-quick reflexes.

Bolan ducked and missed the looping backswing by a wider margin, hearing Cherry's stifled scream behind him. He squeezed off a single silenced round almost into the face of his assailant.

And he recognized the sound of impact into flesh and bone, a heartbeat was left to see the first shape melt away before its partner came straight for him, snarling like an animal, the knife arm arcing down toward contact.

Bolan rolled away, relying on the fallen door to trip his second enemy, and helped out with a parabellum mangler that took off a fist-sized section of his adversary's skull. The body slithered down beside him, fairly oozing in the boneless fashion that no living form can duplicate precisely.

Bolan rose and was moving when he heard the sounds of combat at his rear. Other forms had come upon his companions from behind, emerging from doorways. Several of the enemy were in range now, striking out at Heath and Cherry in the darkness.

Bolan doubled back to help them, saw the woman bring her hatchet down upon a shaven skull with crushing force, then recoil from the strangled cry it produced. Heath Mohawk was grappling with a pair of punkers wielding baseball bats. He slit one from ear to ear before he took a stunning blow across the shoulders from behind. Bolan shot the other batboy and rolled the body free to help Mohawk stand.

"Come on!" he told them both. "We're almost there."

The front doors were no more than ten yards away and Bolan led them on a final sprint for daylight. It was a beat short of too late when he saw the threat.

Filthy curtains parted on a doorway to his right, and a behemoth clad in denim stepped out of the murky cave in which he had awaited them. The biker's big hands dwarfed the sawed-off double-barreled shotgun, which he carried with a kind of practiced self-assurance.

The giant fired his first load high, instinct taking over in the heat of battle. Bolan felt the wind of death brush past him, and he opened fire before the biker had a chance to realize his last mistake. The parabellum crushers punched him backward through the curtain's silent darkness.

And suddenly. . . they were alone.

There was no sound, no hint of movement other than their own inside that corridor of death.

"We did it."

Bolan registered the disbelief within Heath Mohawk's tone. He scrambled to his feet, already moving toward the double doors that opened on the clean night just outside.

"Not yet," he said to both of them, as he threw wide the doors. "Let's save the celebrating till we're clear."

They followed him outside across the wide veranda, now deserted. No sign anywhere of Pink or his companion, and the Executioner spent half a second wondering if they were with the fallen, stretched out back there in the darkened corridors of Hotel Hell.

No matter.

Bolan felt the night air on his face, inhaled it deeply, driving out the musty taste and odor of the Garden Court Apartments. He knew that he had been mistaken.

It was safer out here, right, however marginally, but the night was far from clean. An odor of corruption lingered with him, stronger than the stench he had endured within the walls of Hotel Hell.

There was a lot of cleaning left to do in Hollywood.

A bloody job yet for the Executioner, damn straight.

And he was wasting time.

The three survivors merged with shadow, melted into friendly darkness, and were gone.

10

"I told ya, Cap'n, it's just like some kinda slaughter-house."

Tim Braddock scowled, eyes narrowed in the glare of floodlights that the lab boys had set up to make their job a little easier. It would be hard enough, he knew, to sort out all the bloody bits and pieces without working in the dark. And it was all exactly as the sergeant had described it for him on the telephone.

Hotel Hell, no sanitary refuge at the best of times, had been converted to a goddamned slaughterhouse. The charnel smell was everywhere, almost strong enough to drown out the competing odors offered up by human squalor.

Sweet heaven.

Thirty years in and the whole damned pension waiting for him. Braddock cursed beneath his breath. Thirteen days until retirement, baker's dozen, and with any luck at all he would be able to get through them without running into any hyped-up junkies who would kill a cop before they took a bust, or walking into some damned shoot-out when he stopped to buy the evening paper.

Thirteen days.

And this.

"What have we got?" he asked, not even trying to disguise the weariness behind his words.

"Let's see, that makes a dozen DOAs—no, thirteen—and we're not through looking. Someone tried to give this town an enema, and this is where they stuck the nozzle."

Thirteen corpses. Thirteen days. The Homicide detective was relieved that he did not believe in omens, fate or any of that other psychic horseflop. Grim reality was bad enough.

Braddock and the sergeant stood aside to let a stretcher team get past them in the narrow corridor, their burden stiff beneath a bloodstained sheet. The captain grimaced. From the contour of that linen shroud, it seemed that this one had gone on to his reward without a head.

Sweet holy heaven.

"Have we got an angle?"

His companion shrugged almost as if in apathy, another burned-out street cop who had seen it all.

"You name it. Could have been a drug burn that got out of hand, some kinda gang reprisal. So far we've got two Mongols upstairs, one Hell's Angel and a scumbag wearing Mau Mau colors we've been looking for, let's see here. . ."

Braddock waited, trying not to breathe while his companion riffled through a pocket notebook and finally found the entry he was searching for.

"That's Marcus Dupree, black male, sought on suspicion of homicide, multiple rape." The sergeant closed his notebook, smiled. "Somebody turned him into a canoe."

The captain hoped he did not see approval in the sergeant's smile.

"You getting anything out of your witnesses?"

"We're sorting through it, but it's pretty thin. They either scattered when the shit came down, or else they may have something of their own to hide. A couple of 'em said one man did all the shooting—well, except that mess you saw on your way in. He may have had some backup, but considering the darkness, the excitement—"

"And the fact that all your witnesses are probably still flying high on sixteen different chemicals," the captain interrupted sourly.

"That, too. The only thing we know for sure is that at

least one man stopped by without an invitation, and the bastard wouldn't take no for an answer."

Braddock fished inside his trench-coat pockets for a cigarette and came up empty, cursing underneath his breath. He had been three weeks on the wagon—doctor's orders—but right now he badly needed a smoke.

"Dammit."

At his side, the sergeant misinterpreted his tone.

"The whole town's going crazy, Cap'n. No two ways about it."

Braddock tried to smile, but could not find it in his soul. The town had damned well been going crazy now as long as Braddock could remember, and he had the job of making sure the lid stayed on. No, scratch that; courts and lawyers had already thrown the lid away some fifteen years ago. The best that he could hope for now was to contain the mess that overflowed from inside, a rancid, reeking spill that fanned out wider every day, corrupting everything it touched.

The so-called civilized society.

"One man," the captain said, speaking to himself.

"Affirmative."

"All right. We know he didn't do the punker with the 12-gauge facial, but he did take out the gunner. So, who else?"

"Well...all of 'em, I guess," the sergeant answered, frowning in his puzzlement.

"Does it make sense that someone with the hardware this dude hauls around would carve your Mau Mau? Would he stop to renovate that other scumbag's brain pan with a hatchet?"

"Hell, I don't... Hey, you mean his backup?"

Braddock nodded.

"Work on that end. I don't believe that one man came here cold without some kind of contacts, and then turned the whole dump upside down."

One man.

Tim Braddock was not buying that one for a second. Not with all the carnage he had seen inside. For one man to do all of that, the guy would have to be a regular—

The captain stopped himself just short of spelling out the name.

Why not? There's nothing to be scared of.

So why did he feel different, almost squeamish, every time he thought about the name Mack Bolan?

It had nothing in the world to do with violence, Braddock knew that much. The sight of blood no longer moved him, though he sometimes felt a pang for certain victims, certain crimes. Despite the years of learning not to care, he still felt something now and then...but it was not the bloodshed in itself. No way.

It was almost a homesick feeling, as an aging man might feel when he drives by the high school where he played and studied as an adolescent. A sensation of something lost beyond recall, no matter how damned bad you wished that you could get it back.

"Let's go get some air," the captain said, already moving, brushing past a team of paramedics loading more dead meat onto a stretcher.

Tim Braddock reached the porch and took a deep breath of the night, content to let the smog erase that other odor from inside. Perhaps a little fresh pollution in the lungs might do the trick and clear his head, prevent an old man near retirement from reliving days of fire and blood with something like fond nostalgia.

But the feeling lingered, nagging at him from a dusty corner of his mind. A sense of loss...and something else.

Guilt, perhaps.

The Homicide detective knew that he had nothing to feel guilty over. Not in Bolan's case or in the countless others he had worked across the intervening years. He did his best on each job, worked every goddamned angle in the books to bring the killers down.

Bolan was a killer, no doubt about it. It had been Tim Braddock's job to hound the youthful soldier out of town, to see his sidekicks dead or locked away, and never mind the fact that Bolan had done more to clean the sewers of Los Angeles in one short, hellfire visit than the best Homicide detectives could accomplish in a lifetime. Hell, a dozen lifetimes.

So Braddock felt nostalgia of a sort, and guilt, however misdirected. And he wondered just exactly how he might react if Bolan was in town today, right now, about to launch another of his lightning sweeps and take out several dozen cannibals along the way. Would Braddock stand back watching while the firestorm ran its course? Or with his thirteen days remaining, would he risk it all to stand in Bolan's way?

Would he, for God's sake, have the courage it would take to help and see the cleanup through?

"I need a smoke," he said to no one in particular, and lumbered off the porch of Hotel Hell in the direction of his unmarked squad car.

It was all bullshit, anyway, he told himself. Mack Bolan was not in Los Angeles. Braddock knew that what he had here was just another overflow of human sewage poisoning the mainstream. Maybe he would find the necessary antidote before his thirteen days ran out.

And if he didn't, well, there would be someone else to follow after him and take up where he had left off. Hell, there was always someone else.

Somehow that thought did not console Tim Braddock.

11

Madam Rita paused before the full-length mirror, scrutinizing her reflection in the glass before she turned away. Not bad for forty, she decided; even better for her *real* age, which was strictly confidential.

Rita thought she could milk the magic forty for a few more years, as long as she kept up a regimen of exercise and watched her diet. Maybe have the doctor take a tuck around the eyes next summer, if those laugh lines got much funnier.

And still, not bad.

It had been years since looks had really mattered to the customers, but Madam Rita had an ego to protect, and she had been on top for too long to let herself go now. She knew she could still attract the johns if she wished. The ones who caught her eye, that is, and had the look of cultured men who might respect experience more than they valued firm young flesh.

As Pasadena's wealthiest and most-respected whorehouse madam, Rita liked to see herself as catering to the cream of L.A. County. She had businessmen and politicians in her trick book, not a few policemen—ones with rank—and a handful of the Bible-thumping clergy who could not pursue their fantasies at home.

Her patrons paid for quality and variety, and Rita made damned sure that each one got his money's worth—money that kept rolling in.

It didn't all remain with Rita, naturally. Apart from the usual overhead, there were all those off-the-record costs that helped her stay in business. She was paying off police, the sheriff's office, anyone who had the power to make it miserable for a working girl. Then there was the local Family's cut—a healthy mouthful—but Rita never argued when the bagman came around on payday. She considered the alternatives, the lethal "accidents" reserved for those without insurance, and she wrote off her premiums as cheap.

Madam Rita's house of joy was situated in a residential district of large estates set well back from the road behind manicured lawns. The neighbors showed no interest in what she did behind closed doors, and there would be no protest as long as her customers kept arriving in their chauffeured limousines and sleek Mercedes. Keep up with appearances, preserve the all-important value of the property, and everything was fine.

Until today.

There was no premonition of disaster to forewarn the aging madam as she descended the curving stairway into the massive parlor that comprised three-quarters of the ground floor. It was early yet for customers, and Rita scanned the three men seated at the bar, still warming up with drinks and getting down to basic conversation with her "hostesses."

One of them was a regular, the other two Orientals, and the madam knew there must be some important merger in the works if they were bringing in the Eastern competition now to get their asses hauled.

She didn't care, so long as someone paid the tab.

She was about to treat the early birds and let them buy her one of several drinks required to get her through the morning when the tall doors leading to the dining room burst open and a vision out of some Marine Corps training film barged in.

The man was tall and probably good-looking in a rugged sort of way beneath his mottled war paint. But for now the brothel owner's eyes were busy taking in the weapons that he carried about his person. Holstered pistols on his hip and underneath one arm, the rigging worn on top of camouflage fatigues, and he was holding a stubby submachine gun in one hand, the deadly muzzle sweeping back and forth to pin them all exactly where they were.

One of the Orientals decided to run, and he was breaking for the entry hall before his two companions had a chance to stop him. Almost casually the soldier brought his burp gun up and stitched a line of neat precision holes across the parlor wall, perhaps a foot above the runner's head. He hit the floor and hugged the carpet, praying in his native tongue.

The madam's first reaction was outrage at how this stranger had defaced her plush designer wallpaper, and then it struck her that the decorator's bills were nothing if he turned the gun her way.

She heard the sound of running feet on the staircase and knew at once that it was trouble. Tommy Shanks, her live-in bouncer and ''security consultant,'' was responding to the gunfire. She saw the soldier turn to meet him even as she turned herself, one arm upraised, her lips already forming words of caution that she knew were wasted.

Tommy had his pistol out, and he was already tracking onto target when the soldier's weapon rattled off another burst. Tommy seemed to disintegrate, bits and pieces of him outward-bound before his brain could get the message. Impact drove him backward, bounced him off the wall before he took a header down the stairs.

The hand upon her shoulder made her flinch, and Rita spun around to find the soldier standing not two feet away from her. She smelled the gun's smoke clinging to him like an air of death and wrinkled up her nose unconsciously. The cold blue eyes stared back at her like chips of ice set in the painted countenance.

Rita almost bolted when he reached for her, until she saw the shiny object in his outstretched hand and sensed he

did not plan to kill her as he had killed Tommy Shanks. Her fingers trembled as she took the marksman's medal from him, held it up to catch the light.

"I'm here," he told her simply, enigmatically. "I'm looking for the Iceman. And the heat stays on until I find him."

Just that, nothing more, and Madam Rita found herself still rooted to the spot, still staring stupidly at his retreating back until the tall doors closed behind him, breaking the spell.

And it was only then that she began to scream.

BOLAN PARKED HIS RENTAL CAR uprange and spent a moment making ready to go EVA. He double-checked his weapons and ammo, made sure the Uzi's sling was comfortable on his shoulder, granting access to his side arms in case of need. One final glance at his combat makeup in the rearview mirror and he exited the vehicle.

The Executioner was striking in broad daylight, right, and advertising his activities—but only to a point. He meant for certain people to find out he was in town, but he would not give up the vital anonymity that was all that kept him alive from one day to the next.

There were the psychological effects to think of, also, and the jungle fighter knew from long experience that war paint, whether camouflage or otherwise, was good for many things besides concealment. Things such as scaring people when the chips were down, and lone warriors needed every edge at their disposal.

He backtracked, following a six-foot wall that ran around the rough rectangular perimeter of his intended target. Built for privacy, the wall was tall enough to put off casual intruders, but it had not been constructed with the Executioner in mind. Bolan pushed the Uzi back across one shoulder, scaled the barrier and touched down in a combat crouch beneath the shady trees inside.

It took him sixty seconds to locate the house, with daylight and the lack of any serious security precautions on his side. He was counting on surprise to delay response time and keep everybody off the phones until he could beat a quick retreat.

Besides, the people he was looking for would be reluctant to invite police inside their sanctuary.

Street talk had told him that the party would be in its third straight day with only diehards left on site. The Executioner was counting on the combination of fatigue, intoxication and sheer stomach-wrenching fear to let him get the drop on anyone who might offer opposition when he showed himself.

He crossed a wide veranda, passing through glass sliding doors that had been left wide open, plush drapes billowing against the breeze. The soldier opened yet another door to find himself inside a sort of giant, sunken living room.

And he had found the party, right.

About a dozen souls were scattered around the room in various conditions of undress and near unconsciousness. The stereo was throbbing out a heavy-metal number, but the inlaid dance floor at the far end of the room was deserted. And no one seemed to notice the Executioner's arrival.

He swiveled toward the stereo, swung the little Uzi up and fired from the waist. The music died, replaced briefly by a crackling sound, the death knell of technology confronted with brute force.

And sudden, ringing silence in the aftermath of gunfire.

Bolan had them now, the ones who were still semiconscious, anyway. He scanned the faces, frightened and sobering reluctantly. Wide eyes were turned in his direction, staring. Some of them were recognizable: a rock star on the velvet sofa and an athlete slouched against the wet bar in a corner. He did not know or care to know the others.

DYNAMITE OFFER

4 EXPLOSIVE NOVELS PLUS SUNGLASSES

FREE

**delivered right to your home
with no obligation to buy — ever**

12

Cornelius Murphy was a pimp. He saw it as an honorable line of work, although the work was mostly done by others now that he had reached a certain level of success. His main job now was trolling for new meat around the Greyhound depot, and it let him dress fine and show off the jewelry his foxes had worked long and hard to pay for.

Mother Africa appeared to be unsullied in Cornelius's blood, his features, but the last name that he carried was the source of considerable irritation.

He had grown up with jokes about "black Irish" until they were coming out his ears, until he learned to stand up for himself and ram that "humor" right back down their throats.

At one point, he had considered entering the Muslim movement as a means of throwing off his "slave name," but the combination of their strict religious principles and Murphy's ego—he could not abide surrendering his own identity to be Cornelius X—had kept him from the plunge. Instead of Allah, he had found the streets, and no one out there gave a damn about your name as long as you were able to produce.

Cornelius Murphy was a prime producer, specializing in the kind of wholesome, farm-bred female flesh that residents of Hollywood were always hungry for.

Murphy drank his breakfast every day at noon in Papa Joe's, a bar on Wilshire Boulevard that catered to the players and their ladies. Paying johns were also not discouraged by the management, which stood to earn a kickback from liaisons made on premises.

At noon Cornelius was sitting in quiet conversation with a quartet of his friends, all gentlemen of leisure, working on his second vodka collins. Cornelius's eyes were on the underpopulated bar, where Wanda Jean, top lady in his stable, was jawing with the lunchtime barkeeper. Cornelius tried to catch her eye without appearing to have noticed how long she was sitting there while the trade went by outside.

Another minute and he would have to have a little talk with Wanda Jean. Might have to touch her up a bit, too, just to make sure he had her full attention before he ran it down about the laws of economics, supply and demand.

Cornelius Murphy was considering the best way to excuse himself, deciding that the other gentlemen would understand and sympathize from past experience with foxes of their own, when a new arrival entered Papa Joe's.

A white man.

And big. A tall, athletic-looking mother.

Cornelius took one look and knew that he was not a john. He did not have the anxious, hungry look that spoke of need, desire. He moved like someone who had come to take instead of buy.

And that spelled cop, but then again...

There was a military bearing in his movements, but at the same time there was something definitely unofficial in his style. Cornelius Murphy finally decided that the stranger was that rarest of endangered species found in Hollywood: a honkie with a death wish.

Brushing past the bar and Wanda Jean, the white man came directly to the corner table where Cornelius and his friends were seated, each pimp staring at him with fine disdain. The cat was on their turf, and if he did not have a badge somewhere inside that flashy suit, he was about to make the biggest and most painful error of his life.

The dude stood above them, hard eyes boring into each in turn, until the closest of them, a Jamaican called King Solomon, got tired of waiting.

"What you want here, man?" he asked.

The big guy slid a hand inside his jacket, and Cornelius waited for the badge to flash, disturbed that he had not been able to identify the cop for what he was. Except there was no badge. The hand came out empty, pausing overhead, the fingers opening until a smallish silver object tumbled out and landed with a clank among the glasses.

Cornelius stared at it for a moment, trying to identify the object. It was like a cross—a kind of medal, obviously—with a circle in the middle of it like some sort of target. It looked familiar, but he could not place it before King Solomon distracted him.

"That s'pose to be some kinda joke, white meat?"

The dude pinned him with those graveyard eyes and said, "I'm looking for the Iceman. Spread the word."

King Solomon just grinned from his chair. So bad.

"The word, my ass. The on'y thing I'm gonna spread around here is yo' face."

And he was moving, rising from his chair like taut spring steel uncoiling, but he was not nearly fast enough. The white man went inside King Solomon's right cross, driving an elbow hard against the Jamaican's ribs, inside the velvet vest. On the backswing, stony knuckles crushed the player's nose, releasing two thin jets of blood that stained his ice-cream suit.

The other pimps moved as one, springing from their chairs and going for the stranger in a blind mad rush. He saw it coming, though, and caught their table with a roundhouse kick that dumped it into Murphy's lap, preventing him and his companions from completing their offensive move.

Sugarman, a tall, thin, almost-star of college basketball, was on his feet before the rest, unlimbering the long blade of an ivory-handled razor that he whipped out of an eelskin boot. He circled his adversary, but the guy never budged, just stood there watching with a calm, contemptuous expression on his face.

Sugarman moved in, and Cornelius thought he had a chance until he saw the burly bastard grasp Sugar's razor wrist, twisting hard until the bones cracked audibly and lifeless fingers dropped the weapon. With his arm straight out and rigid, Sugarman was vulnerable to the crushing elbow that slammed down into his own, and he could only squeal in agony as cartilage gave way, his arm snapped backward like a turkey wishbone.

The rest of them were on their feet now, intent on punishing this white man for his impudence and salvaging their sullied honor in the process. Murphy circled to the left with Charley Waters, while their good friend Mojo faded to the right. With any luck they could confuse this bad-ass honkie, catch him in a pincer movement and stomp him into the ground.

But all the luck they had that noon was sour, dammit, and Cornelius knew he was in trouble when the cat took out Mojo with a single snap kick to the face, almost decapitating him.

The invader turned to face them, never hesitating as he closed the gap. And he was smiling, for cryin' out loud, like a goddamned crazy man as he advanced with almost casual strides. He might have been out strolling in the freaking park instead of fighting for his life inside the baddest pimp bar on South Wilshire.

Cornelius wished he had not left his piece at home, but wishing couldn't help him now. In fact, it looked as if there would be more spilled blood in another second. And it would be his unless he found a way to stop this super-honkie from annihilating him.

Murphy brushed against a fallen chair, and he was stooping down to grab it when, beside him, Charley Waters made his move. The little pimp let go a rebel yell that came out twice his size, and then he rushed the white man, both arms flailing like a windmill, totally devoid of any strategy. The stranger stepped aside to let him pass, then clipped him with an openhanded chop behind the ear that drove him on into a facefirst confrontation with the bar.

Murphy had the chair now, and he swung it overhead. He was halfway to his target when a flying boot came out of nowhere, burying its steel-capped toe in Murphy's genitals. He doubled over, gasping silently, and scarcely felt it as his own damn chair came down across his shoulders. He was dying, definitely, and he did not care, as long as sweet extinction took away the pain.

A strong hand grasped his shoulder, turned him over on his back, and bright new waves of pain assaulted Murphy's abdomen. Through blurry tears, he looked up into eyes as cold as death itself.

"I'm looking for the Iceman," his assailant said again. "I'll be around until I find him. Spread the word."

Cornelius Murphy tried to nod a weak affirmative, and vomited instead. He cupped his throbbing testicles in both hands, drawing up his knees until they met his chest, protecting wounded organs in a fetal curl.

He might not die, at that, the pimp decided, but it would be days, at least, before he had the wherewithal to do his ladies any good or look in on the Greyhound station. What he needed was a rest from all this leisure, and he planned to take a long vacation just as soon as he could pick his ass up off the floor.

But first he had to spread the word.

THE YOUNG DIRECTOR BENT DOWN, trying for a different angle of attack and finally getting it, gesticulating for the cameraman to follow him. The lights were hot despite the air conditioning inside the warehouse set; their heat had put a sheen of perspiration on the three slim bodies intertwined before him, writhing on a rumpled bed.

"Right here," he told the cameraman. "Get this and zoom in for a close-up when he makes his move."

The director decided that the cameraman was cool, professional, almost indifferent to the sexual athletics that filled his lens. Some of them got so wrapped up in their work they lost perspective, ruined shots. The director hated working with those types, but given a professional...

He cherished no illusions that the films he made were art. They paid the bills, and when he had to think about it for extended periods of time, he told himself that it was just a phase, a stepping-stone to something bigger, better. But in the meantime...

"All right, Dan, time for action."

And the "actor" glanced up at him, heedless of the camera that recorded every move and left him looking like exactly what he was: a brainless piece of meat, on hold and waiting for instructions.

He watched the so-called actor as he moved into position. Then suddenly everything exploded around him. Klieg lights on the young director's left and right erupted into hissing, sizzling sparks, and it was only after that he heard the thunder, rolling in from somewhere on his flank like cannon fire.

He spun around and saw an apparition dressed in black approaching, one arm up and out in front, the big hand wrapped around a silver handgun that was unlike anything the young director could remember. Smoke was curling from the muzzle, and the cannon's mouth, a black, unflinching eye that pierced his soul, was aimed directly at his face.

A stifled scream from one girl on the bed, and then the actor made his break, stark naked as he hit the floor and ran for daylight.

The armed intruder moved another long stride closer, handgun never wavering from its selected target.

"Listen, man..."

"You listen," the intruder told him, cool and calm.

"I'm looking for the Iceman. Spread the word. Somebody knows where I can find him. Nothing moves until I do."

"I hear you, guy."

The young director heard, all right. And understood.

He knew the Iceman, rather, knew about him, as the children of the streets know every hero-villain—by his reputation. This one was unsavory and dangerous, the kind who liked inflicting pain for either fun or profit. And, they said, the Iceman had devised a way to merge the two.

He "knew" the Iceman, then, although the two of them had never met. And there was nothing he could tell this fierce-looking man in black, except to parrot what he had already said.

"I hear you."

Yeah.

He heard.

And if he lived beyond the next few heartbeats, he would do as he was told.

His cameraman had spun around at the first sound of gunfire. He stood staring at the black-clad apparition with his camera running, just as if the action had gone on uninterrupted, which it had, in some almost demented way. The young director felt as if he had been lifted off the porno set and put down in the middle of a documentary on sudden death.

And he devoutly hoped it would not be his own.

The man in black appeared to see the camera for the first time, grimacing beneath his camouflage cosmetics.

"You won't need that film," he said, swinging the silver cannon toward the camera, squeezing off another thunderclap before the young director had a chance to flinch.

He actually heard the bullet, it was that close to his ear, and there was no way on this earth that he could miss the crash behind him or the screaming of the cameraman as supersonic lead drilled through his lens, exploding on the inside to eviscerate the camera. As he watched, dumbfounded, shiny loops of film came spilling out, exposed and useless now, like the intestines of a dying robot.

"Remember," Grim Death told the young director, turning slowly, showing them his back as he retreated toward the nearest exit.

If I had a gun, he thought. . . and stopped himself.

Then I'd be dead. No doubt whatever on that score.

He watched the gunman disappear: an open door; the sudden glare of sunlight from without—then nothing. And the young director knew he had to reach a telephone without delay.

He had to tell someone about the Iceman.

13

Vincent Andriola took another sip of wine and waited for the alcohol to start relaxing him. It was his private stock, a favorite vintage, and yet today it tasted sour, rasping on his palate, doing nothing yet to soothe his nerves.

The *capo* of Los Angeles was not accustomed to the feeling of inadequacy that had stalked him through this morning. He had grown used to giving orders, solving problems with a word, a knowing glance, but now that things were seemingly beyond his personal control, the mobster was experiencing old and half-forgotten feelings that he did not care to name.

Like doubt.

Like impotence.

Like fear, goddammit.

And which man in his right mind would not be afraid of the recurring nightmare that was haunting Vince Andriola after all this time. Which man could watch the strong foundation of his empire start to crack beneath him without questioning himself, his manhood?

Andriola's hand was shaking as he reached for the wineglass. He brought it back, thrusting a tight fist into the pocket of his lounging robe. He cursed himself for weakness, and he cursed the circumstances that had brought this plague upon him now.

He paused before the full-length mirror set into a corner of his private study, coldly scrutinizing his reflection in the glass. At forty-seven he could pass for ten years younger if he tried, and there was steel yet in the eyes, the backbone.

Satisfied that nothing of his inner doubt was visible to others, Andriola faked a smile and turned away.

If he could just control the trembling of his hands.

A soft, insistent rapping at the outer door, and Andriola cleared his throat before answering it.

"Come in."

The houseman poked his head inside the study, frowning at the *capo*'s back, and said, "He's here."

"All right."

He kept up a pretense of studying the bookshelves until he heard the door open, ease shut again. He wrinkled his nose as Bobby Benedetto's strong cologne filled the room.

The underboss was standing near the door trying not to stare as Andriola turned around. He took a moment sizing Benedetto up and noted that the crisis had not cramped his style. The younger man was smartly dressed, like something off the cover of an all-male fashion magazine, a little half smile on his suntanned face.

He was like a goddamned mannequin, the *capo* thought. A mannequin with strong cologne. No casual observer would suspect that Benedetto stood as second-in-command and heir apparent to the largest Mafia family this side of the Mississippi.

"Want some wine?"

"Too early."

My ass, thought Andriola sullenly. I only hope it's not too late.

"So, have a seat," he said, attempting to suppress the tension in his voice.

The underboss slid into a leather-covered armchair, crossed his legs and relaxed. "I understand we've got a little problem," Benedetto said before his boss could bring the subject up himself.

The *capo* raised an eyebrow. "Little? Just exactly what would you consider serious, huh, Bobby?"

Benedetto did his best to look contrite, but it was far from a convincing act.

"You know that isn't what I meant, Vince," he replied. "I'm just as hot about this thing as you are, but we can't get spooked because some asshole renegade decides to do a kamikaze number on us."

"You think that's the answer, do you, Bobby? Just some head case with a death wish running wild in Hollywood?"

"What else?" The underboss's shoulders lifted in a lazy shrug. "We've seen this kind of thing before. Some guy with more damn guts than brains decides to play the big leagues, and this time next week he's a memory."

"You're on it, then?"

His second-in-command looked startled, then insulted by the question.

"Sure, I'm on it. You think I write off five hits like it's nothing? Hell, Vince—"

"That's six," the *capo* interrupted him. "I got a call from Danny Maranzano a short time ago. It was a little hard to understand him with the sirens and all. Seems like the cops and arson squad are picking through some ashes over where his shopping center used to be. You know, the one on La Cienega?"

And Bobby Benedetto was not smiling anymore. In fact, his frown was carving furrows in the suntan, and his lips were white.

Andriola knew his underboss owned a piece of Maranzano's "shopping center," which amounted to a skin-flick theater, a porno shop and some associated enterprises clustered beneath a common roof. He had, in fact, established it himself some years before, when he was on the rise and just beginning to stake out his territory in the fields of drugs and sex. He had pulled down a handsome income from the two, but now the depredations of the man he called a renegade were hitting Benedetto where it hurt the most. His bankroll.

The *capo* of Los Angeles could sympathize, but he could not escape the feeling that there was much more to this than money. A chilling sense of déjà vu had settled over him that morning as he listened to the string of calls from frightened, angry representatives around L.A., and he could not escape the feeling that he had been through it all before.

"You still think what we're looking at is just some renegade? Some psycho?" Andriola made no effort to conceal the skepticism in his tone.

His underboss put on a blank expression, looked confused. "What else?" he asked. "No other Family is gonna mess with us this way. It don't make sense."

The *capo* sighed, a whisper of his disappointment. "Nobody said anything about another Family."

"Then what? I mean, who else—"

"You heard about this bastard's calling card?"

The frown was back on Benedetto's face. "Some kinda medal?"

"Not some kind. A marksman's medal," Andriola told him. "That put you in mind of anything?"

It took another moment, but the underboss was getting there. His frown was lifting, rapidly retreating as he took on an expression of bewilderment.

"Hey, Vince, you don't mean—"

"Don't I?"

And Bobby Benedetto had it now, but he was not prepared to buy it yet.

"What makes you think the guy's in California? Hell, I mean, what makes you think the bastard's still alive?"

"You read the papers, Bobby?" Andriola asked sarcastically.

"Not much," the underboss responded.

"You think they made up old Phil Sacco's trouble down in Florida? And what about that frigging mess in Vegas?"

"Way I heard it, Sacco couldn't get a handle on the

Cuban situation. Too damned old to pull his weight, would be my guess." The *capo* wondered if he heard a warning beneath the younger man's words. "The Vegas crowd ran up against some Japs and that old relic—what was his name?"

"Abe Bernstein."

"Right. They shoulda punched his ticket twenty years ago, for chrissake. They were sitting on a goddamned time bomb and they didn't even know it."

"There were marksman's medals in Miami," Andriola told him softly, waiting for the impact of his words to register.

But Benedetto never flinched.

"I heard that story," he replied. "It doesn't sound so funny with all the paramilitary bullshit that the spics go in for. And they didn't find no medals in Las Vegas."

Andriola's hands were shaking once again, as much from anger and frustration as from nerves. It seemed that Benedetto was deliberately dense, as if he sought to taunt his own superior, expose the *capo* for a sniveling coward.

"Never mind what anybody found or didn't find in Vegas," Andriola said, his tone like ice. "I'm telling you this feels like Bolan, and I want you on your toes."

It was the first time he had voiced the name in. . . what? How many years? And he could feel another presence in the study with them now, as if by speaking that one word he had invoked a hostile spirit from the other side of hell, invited it to move in with him here and make his life an endless waking nightmare.

Bolan.

Andriola had seen the bastard once—or thought he had—back in the days when Vince was still a small-time soldier working under Julian DiGeorge. The *capo* of Los Angeles was one of the minority who walked away with skin intact. The sheer attrition of those hellfire days had marked the upward path for Andriola, cleared others from the field whom he could never have outlasted or defeated on his own.

The mafioso harbored no illusions as to his abilities. He was a competent administrator, adequate at keeping peace or making war, depending on the need, but he was sure as hell no Deej. Not by a damn sight.

And Mack Bolan had defeated Deej.

Not once, dammit, but twice.

What would he do with Vincent Andriola?

"What?"

The sound of Benedetto's voice startled Andriola out of his private reverie. He made up for his embarrassment by scowling at his underboss, pretending that his mind was occupied with weighty matters far beyond the other's comprehension. Which was very nearly true, at that.

"I said I'm on my toes already, Vince. This bum's been operating. . .what, twelve hours? My bet is he'll never make it twenty-four."

"I hope you win that bet," the *capo* told him sourly.

"It's in the bag."

"Don't count your chickens, Bobby."

Benedetto thought about it, grinned, then finally laughed out loud, a barking sound that grated on the nerves.

"That's pretty good, Vince. Have to keep that line in mind."

The elder mafioso took a moment to catch up with Benedetto, finally remembering that "chicken" was the street term used for children employed as prostitutes or pornographic models.

"Just keep in mind what I've been telling you, goddammit!" And his sudden vehemence was all it took to sober Bobby Benedetto. "No renegade pulls off the kind of crap we've had around L.A. these past few hours. No Cuban, no damned Japanese, no man from Mars. You understand? One man, one soldier who's worth fifty of the best we've got!"

The *capo* felt himself begin to tremble, heard the cracking of his voice and made a conscious effort to retrieve his slipping dignity. Across from him, his underboss sat silent in the leather-covered chair, regarding Andriola as he might a sideshow denizen, with mixed uneasiness and awe.

"I hear you, Vince," the younger mafioso said when he could find his voice. "Don't get excited. I've got men out now. They're doing everything they can to trace this guy."

"I hope it's good enough. For your sake, Bobby."

Benedetto paled a shade beneath his tan, but made no reply. When Andriola rose, his underboss got up and moved in the direction of the study door, no longer comfortable in the small, confining room.

The *capo*'s voice arrested him with one hand on the doorknob.

"Don't let this one get away from you," he cautioned. "If I'm right, you won't get any second chance. If I'm wrong... we still can't let this bastard walk away."

"He won't be walking anywhere when I get through with him," the underboss replied, half turning from the door. "You've got my word, Vince."

"No more time for words," he said. "I need results."

His second-in-command accepted the dismissal silently and closed the study door behind him.

Alone again, Vince Andriola hurriedly refilled his wineglass, drained it in a single swallow and went back for more.

If he was right about Mack Bolan there were still some nagging questions to be answered. Like this message that the goddamned guy kept leaving every time he made a hit. Some crap about an ice man. And just what the hell was that supposed to mean? He had not posed the question to his underboss, preferring to inquire about the matter on his own while Bobby concentrated on protecting their investments in the streets. He should be all the more protective since every target hit so far had fallen squarely in his own backyard.

If he was right, they were looking at a firestorm like none other the town had seen since Bolan last blew in.

If he was wrong—please, God—then there was still a problem, but at least one that he might have a chance to solve.

The *capo* of Los Angeles did not intend to go out like his old boss, Deej, cut down by some barbarian who didn't know the rules. Vince Andriola owned the game, and if Bolan wanted to invade his turf, cut through Los Angeles a second time, it just might be the worst mistake he ever made.

The wine was taking hold at last, and he could feel the tension slowly leaking out of him. A sidelong glance took in his own reflected profile in the full-length glass, and Andriola thought that he looked strong, majestic, the way a mafioso was supposed to look.

He would let Bobby Benedetto work the streets awhile, see what he could come up with, and if something broke that needed older, wiser hands, he was available. To hell with all of that inadequacy crap. To hell with Bolan. The *capo* had an army on his side and all the odds were in his favor. Bolan—if it was Mack Bolan—had no further tricks secreted up his sleeve.

The soldier was a has-been, looking for a place to die, and Andriola's town would do as well as anyplace.

In fact, he thought, it might be better.

It would be poetic justice if he could take the bastard out right here, where Bolan had waged his first campaign of any real significance and scored his big points against the brotherhood. No other *capo* could contest his right to run the L.A. Family then, not with the Bolan scalp to prove his worth.

It must be Providence, the *capo* of Los Angeles decided, that had brought Mack Bolan back to him, providing him a second chance to make the kill-shot he had never tried to make that dark night at Balboa.

Hell, it must be fate.

14

Los Angeles was simmering by noon. According to the DJ doubling as weatherman, the temperature was flirting with a new record and was expected to climb higher in the next few days. Impatient now, Mack Bolan killed the radio as he turned west onto Sunset.

There were other kinds of heat in Hollywood this afternoon, and weather was the least of Bolan's worries as he made a quick preliminary driveby of his new objective. The Executioner had been applying heat all night and through the morning, waiting for the pot to boil, and he was not alone. Detectives out of Homicide, enforcers for the syndicate, a group of angry, battered pimps on Wilshire Boulevard—all were turning up the flame in their respective kitchens, working on the ingredients of a devil's brew, which, when added to the final recipe might be explosive.

And warrior Bolan desired to help them toward that flash point. He was fuse and detonator for the time bomb ticking in Los Angeles, but so far he had no concrete idea of where Ground Zero lay. He had been traveling a violent zigzag course these past few hours, playing hunches for the most part, virtually devoid of guidance. Waiting, right, for shock waves he produced to trigger secondary tremors in the underworld and lead him home, directly onto target.

He had a name at last, an address, and had double-checked them back through Cherry Gifford, phoning in to the motel where he had dropped her off.

He hoped it was the last place anyone would look for her

She recognized the name, connected it with distribution of selected "specialties" outside the realm of normal sex films. There was fear and something else—a caring—in her voice as she had asked him to be careful.

Despite the legends that had grown around his exploits, Bolan was no wild-assed warrior, living on the edge and chasing danger for the hell of it. He valued life—all life—and never risked his own unnecessarily. Whenever possible his movements on the battlefield would be preceded by a thorough recon and collection of intelligence. Bolan always sought to tag the enemy, to know his number and his name before committing himself to a firefight situation. But sometimes you simply had to live on instinct and let events select your course.

Sometimes.

Like now.

His first objective was a seedy camera shop. The sallow clerk inside responded to a purchased password and the offer of a hundred-dollar bill. He sold the Executioner a ticket and gave him directions to a private screening scheduled for that afternoon. Admission at the door, he said, would be another thousand dollars. Bolan flashed a chilling, grave- yard smile and told him it was cheap at half the price.

The "theater" was above a pharmacy on Figueroa. Bolan left his rental car in the parking lot out back and made his way inside. He felt a momentary chill as air conditioning washed over him and dried the perspiration clinging to his skin.

He brushed on past the magazine rack, where a clutch of pimply high-school boys were poring over something in the latest *Penthouse*, and homed on the cashier's cage in back. A youngish man was lounging at the counter, watching Bolan with a practiced air of diffidence, one hand invisible behind the showcase. He would have a finger on the panic button, right, prepared to sound a warning if his latest customer turned out to be the heat.

Mack Bolan slid his ticket through a slot in the cage and said, "I'm looking for a Tommy Nash."

"You found him."

Both hands showed above the counter now, his ticket vanishing with a flourish, and the young man met his eyes.

"They told you about the extra fee?"

Bolan nodded, slid one of his G-notes underneath the gate. The young man glanced around, assured himself they were alone, and held the bill up to the light. When he was satisfied that it was genuine, a grin broke out across his boyish face.

"You're in," he told the jungle fighter. "Good thing, too. It's almost show time."

Nash conducted his new patron through a door restricted to Employees Only, along a narrow corridor until they reached a staircase in the rear. They climbed one flight, with Bolan hanging back a pace and ready to defend himself in case of ambush, finally pausing at a door marked Private.

Tommy Nash brushed through it, and the soldier followed him into a smallish room that reeked of perspiration, stale cigars and something else Bolan did not want to name. It was familiar, that odor, from another time and place, composed in equal parts of tension and excitement with a dash of lust.

Eleven men were seated in three rows of folding chairs, their backs toward the door. Some of them swiveled to examine Bolan as he entered, one man nodding to him with a knowing smile, but others kept their eyes fixed upon the blank white wall ahead of them. Nash directed Bolan to the only vacant chair, and as he took his seat, the Executioner was studying the other members of the little audience.

They were dressed in business suits, well-groomed and manicured. Some doctors or attorneys in the crowd, perhaps. A middle-aged executive or two in search of stimulation over and beyond the normal. Bolan had no clear idea just what "specialty" would be displayed for their amusement, but whatever it might be, it was a paying proposition for the house. He did some mental calculations based upon the size of the audience, and realized that with a mere two shows per week the theater would gross in excess of a million dollars a year.

The lights went down and a whirring sound from the projector overhead invaded Bolan's consciousness. Huge, inverted numbers started flashing on the wall in front of him. The numbers counted down from ten in half as many seconds, and were suddenly replaced by what appeared to be the bedroom of a middle-class suburban home.

The grainy color film ran for several seconds before two men appeared wearing crotchless leather pants and ski masks. Between them was a naked girl, perhaps sixteen, supported by the men on either side. From the slack expression on her face Bolan guessed that she had been sedated prior to filming.

He felt his stomach tighten as the masked men laid her down across a queen-size bed, producing dime-store handcuffs that they used to fasten wrists and ankles to the four bedposts. She was held spread-eagled and immobile underneath the camera's eye as the men backed away and took positions somewhere out of camera range.

The old familiar smell was back again, and stronger now. It made the jungle fighter wrinkle his nose and close his mind to memories of fire and thunder. Heavy breathing on his left, and Bolan fought the urge to drive a crushing elbow through the profile of a stranger half his age. This man had paid his thousand dollars to observe the grim debasement of another human being, and his rigid posture told Mack Bolan he was getting every penny's worth.

The girl on screen was undulating slowly, moving as if in response to music that the audience was not allowed to hear. It was a silent film, the projector's soft whirring and the rising tide of heated respiration merging into tawdry sound effects.

It struck the Executioner as strange that anyone would pay a thousand dollars to observe a rape, when everything from bestiality to kiddie porn was readily available at bargain-basement rates. He knew there must be something more in store for this particular performance, but he could not quite prepare himself for what came next.

A slender man appeared on screen, completely nude except for leather chaps and mask, with metal-studded straps across his chest like bandoliers. He was erect and ready as he crawled aboard the bed between his captive's outstretched thighs. He entered her without preliminaries, and the camera started circling the bed, to capture different angles as he plundered her unmercifully.

The girl on screen was fully conscious now, saying something to her masked attacker. Pleading? Screaming? Bolan clenched his teeth and closed his mind to what was happening around him, sounds and subtle movements from the other members of the audience as they fell into step with the performance. Just in front of him, a white-haired man in natty pinstripes had a raincoat folded in his lap, one hand beneath it, working rapidly.

It would be simple, so damned simple to reach out and grasp his head, one hand cupped underneath the chin for leverage. A simple twist...

Mack Bolan almost missed the climax of the film, it came so suddenly, without a hint of warning. The leather mask reached up with one hand, searching, and a tattooed arm materialized beside him, handed him a slim stiletto. And it was as clear as crystal what the man intended to do....

Mack Bolan found the sleek Beretta, ripped it free of leather as he came out of his seat. Gargantuan, his shadow blocked a portion of the screen, left disembodied legs exposed where they emerged beneath one shadow arm. In front of him, the white-haired "gentleman" was swiveling, the raincoat slipping down around his ankles as he croaked in outrage.

"Sit down!"

Bolan chopped the sentence off, his side arm cracking down across the perfect nose and ruining a most expensive face-lift.

Pivoting, he stared directly down the film projector's luminescent funnel for a heartbeat, saw the twisting shapes distorted, merging into forms no longer human. He could hear his own pulse throbbing in his ears as he squeezed off a single parabellum round and closed the glowing eye forever.

Sudden darkness, scrambling figures all around him, and the jungle fighter concentrated on the only one who mattered. Tommy Nash was breaking for it, had the door open before Bolan picked him out among the darting shadows.

Someone blundered out in front of him, and Bolan never broke his stride. A stiff right arm thrust out in front of him connected with the pallid face, and there was only time to register the impact, note the sharp parabola of flying dentures as he reached the exit.

Tommy Nash was at the bottom of the stairs. A few more strides and he would clear the office area, explode into the drugstore proper and the street beyond with all its hiding places, its civilians strolling through the line of fire.

The Executioner took the chance and fired from the hip, relying on training, instinct and the almost point-blank range to compensate for lack of preparation. One short, muffled sneeze from the Beretta, and an empty cartridge casing clinked against the wall beside him.

The parabellum round clipped Tommy Nash's shoulder, spun him around and dumped him facedown on the drab linoleum.

The Executioner was closing on his quarry when a door

banged open overhead, and panicked members of the audience began stampeding down the stairs. He spun around to meet them, the Beretta braced in both hands, muzzle elevated, sighting up the slide and locking onto target even as the startled pointman saw him, recognized his danger.

Grudgingly, the jungle fighter raised his sights another click and pumped two silenced rounds into the ceiling of the stairwell, raining plaster down upon their heads. The stampede faltered, broke, flowed back upstairs and out of sight along the corridor, a couple of the older runners gasping, clutching at their chests in pain.

He wished them all the agonies of hell and left their fate to Mother Nature, moving back downstairs to find his prey. The wounded man had wriggled twenty feet along the blood-slick floor, still trying to outrun his destiny despite the pumping wound. Bolan overtook him in half a dozen strides, caught his ravaged shoulder and flipped him roughly over on his back.

It took a moment for the young man's eyes to focus through his pain, and Bolan held the autoloader close enough for him to see it clearly, smell the acrid smoke clinging to the weapon's muzzle. When he had the guy's complete attention, Bolan spoke to him with tight-lipped fury.

"One time. Where do I find the Iceman?"

"Please, I need a doctor. I—"

The plea became a strangled scream as Bolan's heel came down against the wounded shoulder, grinding splintered bone on bone. He stepped back, bending close once more and waiting for the bleary eyes to find their focus.

"I don't want to ask you twice," he told the maggot, reaching down to press the muzzle of his weapon tight against a forehead slick with sweat. "The Iceman. Now."

"He doesn't deal with me."

And Bolan's heel was poised above the leaking wound when Tommy Nash broke down, his good hand rising, vainly trying to forestall more pain. His voice came out a desperate soprano, strained through mortal terror.

"Wait! I rent the flicks from a distributor in town. From what I hear, he has a pipeline to the guy you want."

"A name."

"D'Andrea. Big John."

"Where do I find him?"

Tommy Nash reeled off an address in North Hollywood.

"What is that?" Bolan asked. "Home? A business office?"

"It's his studio," the wounded man replied. "He takes some clients there, supplies them with some special services. . . oh, jeez!"

The maggot fought a losing battle with his pain, and Bolan spent a moment watching him, remembering the ghoulish spectacle he had observed upstairs. A deep, abiding anger rose out of his gut and set his pulse hammering behind his eyes. Unbidden, his mind brought up the gory image of the woman-child.

"You've been a big help, Tommy," Bolan said. Then he put a single parabellum round between the bleary eyes.

The Executioner straightened, returned the 93-R to its shoulder rigging as he made his way along that corridor of death.

Once more he had a name and an address.

Bolan felt a growing sense of urgency and realized the war was coming home to him again, becoming personal. He saw the Iceman and the other scum who dealt in human degradation as a personal affront to everything he cared about. To life itself, damn right.

And as he cleared the store, emerging into smoggy daylight, Bolan realized that it was always personal. It had been from the start and would be ever more, so long as he possessed the strength to stand and fight.

A *personal* crusade.

Hell, yes.

Society's attempt to compromise with evil, to appease the savages, did not bind any individual against his will. One man could make a difference, providing that he had the guts to stand his ground and draw the line.

Mack Bolan had already drawn the line in Hollywood, and if he stood alone against the cannibals, so be it. He would keep it one-on-one, up close and personal.

The Executioner would not have it any other way.

15

Bobby Benedetto knew he was a lucky man. At thirty-four he was a millionaire, and he stood one step removed from absolute control of every major racket in Los Angeles. He had worked hard, fought hard, to reach his present state, but secretly the mafioso could admit that he owed much of his success to plain dumb luck.

And luck was fragile.

It could turn sour, Benedetto knew, the minute you started taking things for granted. And it could damn well blow up in your face if you got overanxious, pushed too far, too fast.

A fragile thing requiring a measure of respect.

The L.A. underboss respected luck, all right, but he was also conscious of his own abilities. It made him sick to hear the old man sniveling and whining, rehashing all that crap about the old days with DiGeorge and Mack "the Bastard" Bolan.

Andriola had his gears stuck in reverse, and he seemed to be approaching his second childhood, hiding inside his big house from the Bolan bogeyman.

So much the better, then, for Bobby Benedetto's own ambitions. While his "superior" was playing hide-and-seek with shadows, Benedetto would make further inroads into Andriola's private game preserve and set the stage for his ascension to the throne.

But first, there was the problem of this goddamn renegade to be ironed out.

He had already embarrassed Benedetto, cost him

money, and the L.A. underboss would have to end it there. Too much was riding on the play to have some wild card tearing up the streets and bringing down all kinds of heat just when he needed time to fit the final pieces into place.

The mafioso had been working toward this moment all his life, and he was not about to see it jeopardized at this late date by some demented kamikaze warrior out of who-knows-where. He was not buying Andriola's Bolan theory for a moment. But suppose the old man happened to be right for once. So what? It would take more than the appearance of a shell-shocked Green Beret to upset Benedetto's plans.

While still a youth he had realized the power and the draw of sex, become aware that men—and women, too—would pay for it. To share it, watch it, even read about it. He had seen his future as he passed the sleazy bookstores and adult arcades proliferating throughout Hollywood. And Benedetto knew that he had found a way to merge his fantasies with the reality of day-to-day survival.

His introduction to the Mafia had been a problem, but not an insurmountable one. The brotherhood was always looking for young men with potential, selecting those who fit the bill and passing over others who might jeopardize a good thing with their lack of discipline.

And Bobby Benedetto could control himself at need. Like in those early days, when the boss was watching, or when success or failure was riding on his sheer ability to make a rational decision. Then, he had been as cold as ice, stripped of all emotion. But the other times...

He smiled, unconsciously, and let his mind stray for a moment through the black museum of memories he had compiled to keep him company. That portion of his psyche was a dark place echoing with screams, alive with twisted shadows that the eye could not make out...not quite. But Benedetto knew exactly what was in there, and in his private moments he would linger there, reliving some particularly favored episode until the hunger drove him out again in search of prey.

Not often, now, but just enough to keep him satisfied. And anyhow, he had the means to cover up his tracks. Hell, he had even found the means to profit from his own excesses, as he had from the desires and weaknesses of others.

The smile grew broader, then faded as he thought of Foster Price.

He had discovered quite by accident that he was holding film on some attorney's daughter. There had been nothing new in that, and it was not the first time Benedetto found the son or daughter of a wealthy businessman performing in his tawdry flicks. What set this time apart was the announcement of Julie Price's father as a candidate to fill a recent Senate vacancy.

It was the kind of situation Benedetto thrived on, and he had not wasted any time in making contact with the would-be senator. Just time enough to check him out, to analyze the polls that named him as the favorite with voters for his law-and-order stance, his hard-line speeches on the menace of the Mob.

It was perfect.

With leverage Benedetto would not only bag a senator, thereby increasing his prestige within the brotherhood, but he would clear himself a path directly to the throne, as well. With Price beneath his thumb, the vice-lord of Los Angeles could "guide" the senator in his pursuit of hoodlums, making sure that certain undesirables were weeded out while his own operations sailed along uninterrupted.

And chief among the undesirables Bobby Benedetto had in mind was *capo* Vincent Andriola.

The old man was losing it. . . what little grip he ever had. It was no secret Andriola had made it to the throne by sheer default. The brotherhood had granted Andriola squatter's rights and heaved a secret sigh of relief when it was realized that he would make no waves, mount no aggressive forays to recover all the territory lost when Julian DiGeorge bought it in a Bolan blitz.

Bolan. . . .

Benedetto made a low, disgusted sound and pushed the telephone away, across his desk. He had been staring at it now for twenty minutes, since the last call told him that their kamikaze was still out there attempting to dismantle single-handedly what Benedetto and an army had built from scratch.

It had to stop, goddammit. And it *would* stop, even if he had to hit the streets himself. Bobby Benedetto had not come this far to let one psycho with a death wish drive him underground and jeopardize his grand scheme for the future.

He was not buying Andriola's theory for a second. All that crap about Bolan coming back to get him was some kind of flashback to the days when Vince had tucked his tail between his legs and run. Benedetto scowled, remembering the talk that he had heard from other members of the brotherhood. Some of them said Andriola could have ended Bolan's run that night in Malibu, so long ago.

Bobby knew the other leaders of the honored society would not be sad to see Vince go. They had been waiting for the advent of someone with guts enough to force him out, and they would welcome Benedetto's move, although he was not fool enough to think that anyone outside L.A. would help him. He would have to do it on his own, of course, and that was fine. With Foster Price and all the power of a U.S. senator behind him, it would be a piece of cake.

Providing that the politician had not run amok by then. His grandstand play last night at the Topanga studio had been disturbing, though it did not take the would-be *capo* by complete surprise. He had seen fire in Foster Price, and he might have foreseen that there would be some effort by the man to find his daughter, set her free and break the chains that held him fast to Benedetto.

It was predictable.

What *had* surprised the future overlord of L.A. County was the outcome of last night's fiasco. More than a dozen soldiers dead, the studio exposed for what it was, the place crawling with vice cops and detectives. Never mind that they could not trace the joint to Benedetto. That did not bother him at all.

It was the knowledge that Foster Price could not have taken out those soldiers on his own.

On-site security had handled him with swift precision, and they had been acting under Benedetto's orders when they trussed him up, began to carry him away. But what happened after was absolutely unpredictable.

Someone had extricated Price and taken out three crews of slick professionals while he was at it.

Someone cool and deadly.

Someone who knew his business inside out.

Someone who might be ripping up the goddamn streets right now and looking for the Iceman.

Benedetto was not buying Bolan as the kamikaze, not until he had some more proof anyway, some evidence beyond those goddamned marksman's medals that had Andriola so worked up.

But if it was not Bolan, then he had to start from scratch, to look for who and why before the bastard turned up on his doorstep.

Maybe, Benedetto thought, he would get lucky, and the kamikaze soldier would go straight for Andriola.

Maybe. And maybe not.

No point in taking chances when so much was riding on the toss. He had an empire to protect, and if he wanted to defend it from the challenges that would inevitably lie ahead, he might as well start with the here and now. It was a cinch that Chicken Vince would not be leading any troops into the field, not while he thought the Executioner was ripping up L.A. and searching for him everywhere. He would be holed up at his hardsite sweating bullets, waiting for his second-in-command to save the fort.

And Benedetto would not disappoint his nominal superior.

He meant to save the fort. But he would save it for himself, and if that whining coward Andriola had a fatal accident along the way, perhaps an accident that could be blamed on Bolan, for example. . . .

Benedetto had a sudden inspiration, knew at once how he could solve two problems in a single stroke.

The kamikaze soldier had been asking everyone he met about the Iceman. Why? Because he knew the Iceman had some link with Julie Price.

The girl. Of course.

Somehow her old man had put someone on the street to find his little darling, and the hunter did not seem to care what lengths he went to.

Fair enough. The future *capo* of Los Angeles could play that game and teach his opposition lessons in the process.

Everybody wanted Julie Price, it seemed, and Benedetto knew that he could bag them all by giving in, providing them with what they wanted. When they came to get the bitch he would be waiting for them. . . with an army. In one fell swoop, he would remove the kamikaze warrior from the streets and shovel Foster Price right back into the bag where he belonged.

Along the way, he just might get some extra mileage out of Julie Price himself. And why not? He deserved some rest and relaxation after all the work her father's little tricks had put him to.

A flat, reptilian smile replaced the frown on Bobby Benedetto's face, and he was chuckling to himself now as he reached for the telephone. There were arrangements to be made, and he could not afford to waste a minute. The Cecil B. De Mille of slime was on a roll. He had an epic to produce, and he already had the female lead in mind.

16

The Executioner made one quick driveby of the "studio" that Tommy Nash had fingered for him with his dying breath. Bolan found a place to park his rental car around the side.

The place was masquerading as a health spa, but from what he had already learned, Bolan knew that the proprietor was not concerned with keeping anyone in tip-top shape. The dozen or so cars already waiting in a smallish parking lot were Lincolns, Caddys and an odd Mercedes for variety.

And Johnny D'Andrea was catering to money, right.

Sick money.

Bolan recognized the name, and on his short drive over he had called up everything he knew about Big John from memory. There was not much, but what he had provided something of a feel for his opponent.

John D'Andrea.

"Big John."

The street name told him more about the scumbag's size than his position in the underworld. Bolan's mental mug file coughed up an impression of D'Andrea as he had looked some years ago in front of the cameras in an LAPD lineup. Tall and beefy, weighing in at better than 250 pounds, he was a slugger with a simian face who liked to throw his weight around. In his younger days his specialty had been harassing and abusing loan shark "clients" who were tardy with their weekly payments.

Someone like him once had called on Bolan's father

back in Pittsfield, in the days before a private war consumed the jungle fighter's life. And someone like him had first suggested how Mack Bolan's sister could "work off" the family debt by taking to the streets.

A rather different kind of debt was on the warrior's mind now, one that had been paid in blood with interest due. He locked the rental car and forced his mind to the problem of the here and now. He moved back along a narrow alley toward the health spa's entrance.

Clearly, John D'Andrea had come up in the world—at least financially. From pushing pain he had moved on to selling sex, and these days it looked as if his clientele was several cuts above the merchant class he had so loved to terrorize in younger days.

Perversity was in, hell yes. It was a seller's market with some "special service" readily available for every twisted taste.

John D'Andrea had come a long way from the days when he was breaking arms and legs on Wilshire Boulevard.

Bolan pushed in through the tinted double doors and was enveloped by the frosty, air-conditioned atmosphere inside. The health spa's lobby was an antiseptic place with nothing of the sweaty, locker-room atmosphere about it, and he guessed that any sweating done around these premises was going on behind closed doors, in private cubicles reserved for paying clients and their "therapists" of choice.

A smiling brunette lovely in a spandex body suit moved to greet him, a hint of invitation in her eyes. She looked him over, taking measure of the stranger, finally unable to decide if he had come for business, pleasure or a combination of the two.

"Yes, sir," she offered. "May I help you?"

"You could let me see Big John."

A flicker of something behind the eyes, and Bolan knew

he had been pigeonholed. The hint of invitation in the lady's smile had vanished now, replaced by cool efficiency.

"Did you have an appointment, Mr.—"

"Blanski," told her gruffly. "And let's cut the crap, okay? I haven't got all night."

He had already registered the television camera mounted overhead, the staring cyclops eye observing him dispassionately.

The beauty's cool was slipping as she answered him.

"I'm afraid Mr. D'Andrea is with a client at the moment. If you'd care to wait—"

"No good," he snapped. "We're in the middle of a shit storm out there, lady. Now you tell Big John to pull his pants up and get back to business, huh?"

As if on cue, a door behind the counter-showcase opened, and a hulking blond behemoth stepped into the lobby. He, too, was dressed in spandex, but in his case the curves were bulging muscle, massive arms and chest, with thighs as thick around as Bolan's waist.

The bastard was a giant, right, and from the dull expression on his suntanned face, he was not feeling friendly toward the new arrival.

Someone had been watching Bolan's little sideshow on the monitor, and they were sending in the heavies now, deciding that the lady needed reinforcements.

The brunette's smile was rigid, almost carved into her pretty face as she addressed Bolan.

"I'll let Mr. D'Andrea know you're here," she said. "If you'll just go along with Courtney there, he'll show you the way."

Courtney? What the hell, it took all kinds.

Bolan brushed past the girl to reach his escort. Standing like a human mountain beside a door marked Private, Courtney stared down at him with a vague expression of suspicion mixed with irritation. And the jungle fighter knew his guide had not been exercising brains to any great degree.

Bolan snapped his fingers at the giant, scowling.

"Let's go, beefcake. Take me to your leader."

"Mr. Blanski—"

Bolan smiled inwardly at the lady's tone of concern and waved her off without turning around.

"Never mind. We understand each other." Then, to Courtney, "Let's make it today, eh?"

Bolan smiled into the glaring eyes and followed his escort along a corridor with doors irregularly spaced on either side. Instead of names or numbers the doors were different colors, and the soldier surmised that each must serve a different sort of clientele.

Bolan thought he could make out voices issuing from several of the private rooms. A little chill crept up his spine and settled in against the base of his skull, but the warrior shrugged it off and kept his eyes upon the massive, rolling shoulders of his guide.

No time now for unaccustomed squeamishness, hell no. He had already come too far and seen too much to let a tremor rock the hand that held the weapon.

And never mind the ground swell of disgust that welled up from his vitals as he moved along the corridor. Forget about the sick and sorry souls who had parked their luxury sedans out back, away from prying eyes, and paid to have their fantasies made flesh.

He had not come to judge them for their weakness, but to find the slimy Hydra's head and crush it underneath his heel.

The Executioner could spare them pity in his passing, certainly, but they were not his chosen targets. He was hunting for the savages who purchased bodies, ruined souls, inflicted all the tortures of the damned on weak, unwilling victims.

He was searching for the Iceman. And for Big John.

The warrior did not know if Courtney had been sent to stall him, rough him up or lead him straight to John

D'Andrea—and he could not afford the time that it would take to tell. He let the muscle man stay a pace or two ahead as they proceeded down the corridor, and by the time they reached its midpoint, Bolan had his plan worked out.

He slipped a hand inside his jacket, freed the Beretta from its armpit sheath and gripped it tightly in his fist, the safety on. He did not plan to kill the beefy slugger—not unless he had to—but he would need to get the guy's attention.

Rushing up behind his escort, Bolan brought a foot down hard behind the giant's knee, the muzzle of his handgun stabbing deep into the target's lower back and seeking out the soft spot of a kidney. Courtney stumbled, went down on one knee, and hands the size of baseball gloves were reaching behind him, searching for the sudden agony that took his breath away.

The jungle fighter swung his autoloader in a wide flat arc, the butt connecting with a point behind the giant's ear. The impact drove his adversary hard against the nearest wall and left him limp there, gasping through his puzzlement and pain.

Crouched in front of him, Bolan let his adversary see the black Beretta's business end. The big oaf's eyes were crossed as he tried to focus on the weapon, and he finally gave up, regarding Bolan with a glance that was accusatory, almost childlike.

"One time, beefcake," Bolan told him. "Where's D'Andrea?"

"Purple...purple door."

It was the last one down, Bolan saw. It might have been their destination all along, but he did not intend to walk in there against the unknown odds with hulking Courtney at his back. No way.

He stepped back from the body builder, saw the weak move coming just in time to counter it. When Courtney tried to tackle him around the legs, Bolan brought his gun butt down against the shaggy skull, driving home the point until his enemy collapsed facedown upon the floor.

The jungle fighter knelt, feeling for a pulse and finally finding it beneath the ropes of muscle in the giant neck. He backed off, knowing he could finish Courtney now without a sound, and choosing not to.

Sergeant Mercy, right.

Against the savages.

He kept the 93-R in his fist as he approached the far end of the hallway, homing on the purple door. Whatever lay beyond it, he was going in prepared. Carrying the battle to his enemies, and on their own home ground.

He hit the tall door with a flying kick and followed through as it slammed back against the inner wall. The soldier entered in a combat crouch, his weapon searching for a target, anyone or anything that posed a lethal challenge to his entry.

And for just a heartbeat Bolan thought he might have stepped into the middle of a lurid dream.

The door had opened on a massive suite decked out in pinks and violets, from the walls and carpeting to drapes that framed a scenic garden view outside. The tinting of the windows told him it was one-way glass; the occupants could feast their eyes on all outdoors without the fear of being seen by anyone who passed outside.

And it was clear to Bolan in a single glance why they would need the privacy. For every stick of furniture within the room—from chairs and bed to something rather like an operating table—seemed designed for nothing quite so much as kinky sex, in any posture that a fevered mind could conjure up. A pair of fur-lined manacles was hanging from the heardboard of a massive oval waterbed, and from the other bondage gear visible around the room, Bolan knew that certain guests were something less than anxious to accommodate their host and his desires.

Big John D'Andrea was standing naked in the center of

the playroom. But Bolan's mind was on the suite's two other occupants, and it was all that he could do to refrain from shouting out his rage, from pumping hot lead through his target's flaccid gut.

A girl, no more than twelve years old by Bolan's estimate, was seated in an armchair just in front of John D'Andrea, her arms and legs secured to the sturdy chair with leather bindings. On the mobster's other flank, a young boy had been bent over a sort of padded sawhorse, head down toward the floor, wrists and ankles locked in handcuffs.

Both were as naked as the day they came into the world.

Both bodies bore the signs of long abuse, maltreatment at the hands of someone who enjoyed his work.

Someone—some scum—like John D'Andrea, damn right.

"What is all this?" D'Andrea inquired, the high-pitched voice thrown higher yet by fear.

"It's judgment day," the Executioner told him flatly.

And he stroked the Beretta's trigger, watched the hulking mobster's left knee disintegrate into a pulpy spray, the pale legs buckling as he sprawled between the captive children.

Surprise had robbed him of the scream, but John D'Andrea was sobbing now and trying to sit up, trying to reach his mangled knee with hands that trembled spastically. The color from his florid face appeared to have drained from him through the bullet wound, and he was corpse-pale from head to jerking toe as Bolan stood in front of him, his handgun leveled.

It took a moment's knife work to release the girl, and well-placed parabellum shockers cut the young boy's shackles. Both were shaky, verging on the incoherent, but he guided them in the direction of a smaller room adjacent to the first, where he could see some robes and other articles of clothing hanging on the wall. There would be nothing in their sizes, of course, but he could give back something of their shredded dignity, at least, and spare them from the sight of what D'Andrea had coming to him in their names.

When they were out of sight, Bolan turned back toward his wounded enemy, surprised to find that John had ceased his blubbering. He fixed the jungle fighter with a hateful stare.

"You smashed my frigging knee," he snarled.

"Consider it my ante," Bolan told him coldly. "Shall I raise the stakes?"

His weapon was already rising when the mobster threw out both hands, bloody palms extended, panic carved into his face.

"Hey, wait a minute, will ya? We can work it out!"

"No sale," Grim Death replied, and paused a second to divert the handgun's aim before he squeezed the trigger yet again.

Round two drilled through the mobster's outstretched palm, 115 grains of superheated metal boring along the axis of his arm and playing havoc with the bone before it tore free at the elbow. Stunning impact spun the man around and wrenched another strangled cry out of him.

Bolan knelt beside him, holding out his autoloader so that John D'Andrea could see it plainly and know that it was aimed directly at his sweating face.

"I'm looking for the Iceman," Bolan told him simply. "You do business with him. You can give me what I need."

It took a moment for the wounded hoodlum to interpret what his ears were hearing, and a look of comprehension spread across his face.

"You shoot me, and then you ask for favors?" Something like a smile there, underneath the painful grimace. "What's in it for me?"

"Some mercy," Bolan told him simply. "More than you deserve."

"My life," he countered, knowing he had little left to bargain with against this grim intruder. "Let me live, I'll tell you what I know."

The jungle fighter smiled. "All right."

"I want your word," D'Andrea insisted, grimacing through his agony.

"You've got it."

There was a momentary hesitation when he thought the mobster might have undergone a change of heart, but then the voice creaked out again between parched lips.

"The Iceman is Bobby Benedetto, dig it?"

Bolan dug it, sure.

"You're full of crap," he told the wounded thug.

"No, listen, man...I'm serious. There's not a half a dozen people in the city—hell, the country—who could tell you that. I know him, man."

The mobster took a ragged breath.

He played his ace—and sealed his fate.

"He's got a big joint out in Pasadena. Like some frigging smorgasbord. Where do you think I got the chicken, man?"

Mack Bolan did not have to think about it any more than he would have to think about what happened next. D'Andrea could see the pistol as it tracked along his body, silenced muzzle homing on his groin, and he could read his doom on Bolan's face.

"Hey, man, hold on!" he cried. "You promised!"

"I lied," Mack Bolan said.

And squeezed the trigger.

Twice.

The dying mobster was convulsed by pain, his body arched into a bow when the Executioner thrust the hot Beretta's silencer between his ovaled lips and ended it.

Bolan glanced around the room and found a telephone concealed behind a velvet hanging tapestry. He tapped out three different numbers in quick succession. He got an answer on the third one, and informed the desk cop down at vice where he could find the leaking body of one John D'Andrea, along with other evidence sufficient to prove child abuse, enslavement, torture, prostitution.

The officer was asking for his name when Bolan cradled the receiver, and his mind was on the two calls that had brought no answer.

One to Cherry Gifford, at the "safe" motel where he had left her with instructions to stay put.

And one to brother John.

If both of them were somehow out of touch...

The soldier did not let his mind move in search of possibilities and grim alternatives.

He had a hot war on his hands, and there was no damn time to deal with mysteries just now, however close to home they came.

He had the Iceman's name and a tentative location for the next phase of his blitzkrieg.

For the moment, it would have to be enough.

Cherry Gifford scowled in frustration as she checked her watch against the ugly sunburst clock above the motel bed.

"Dammit!"

She had been waiting for LaMancha's call and chafing at the bit, but there had been no contact since he'd called her in the early morning to check on a name and address, and warn her to stay close, stay hard.

She had been learning just exactly what that meant since Frank LaMancha walked into her life last night, and Cherry had a feeling that the lesson was not over yet.

She had been tough before, but there was all the difference in the world between the kind of tough she had been accustomed to and staying hard. Belinda Gifford had been unprepared for last night's action, fighting for her life in the reeking corridors of Hotel Hell. And the wonder of it was that she survived at all.

There had been nothing to compare with that experience in all her not-so-tender years, and if she thought about it, she could still feel the jolting tremor in her forearms as the hatchet bit into a cue-ball skull.

She had killed a man. To save herself. To help LaMancha and the boy, Heath Mohawk. The sickness found her later when she was alone, and she was thankful that the big, broad-shouldered warrior had not been around to see her weakness.

He was a *hard* man, but then again, there had been something underneath the grim exterior....

She thought about the youth and the way he had volunteered to join them in their search, not knowing and not caring what it might consist of. He had tasted battle, tasted freedom, and he was hungry for another slice, but Frank LaMancha had reined him in.

"It's not your fight," he had told Mohawk almost gently, with what sounded like a real trace of regret. "You've done enough."

And he had passed the kid a wad of cash that must have come to several thousand dollars, when they dropped him off a short walk from the Greyhound station. There were no judgments made, no sermons. LaMancha trusted Heath to make his own choice, sensing that the night had changed him somehow, made him older, more mature.

The way it had changed Cherry Gifford.

She wanted to help him, and not just for the sake of some girl she had never passed a hundred words with in her life. Not just because some runaway had people looking for her, grieving for her.

No.

Because she *had* to.

Now that she knew the *hard*, she felt compelled to act, make something of her life besides a quick slide through the underground in Sewer City.

Cherry smiled to herself, knowing she sounded like some kind of Bible-thumper. But it wasn't like that, not at all. Her revelation was a private one and strictly personal. She had to take some action for herself, and not for anybody else.

But there was still LaMancha's order for her to stay close, and Cherry did not dare leave the motel room in case he called again. Five hours passed before she started thinking through the problem from her own perspective, seeking angles that she could attack alone, and she stayed close, connecting with assorted friends and contacts on the telephone, extracting bits and pieces of the puzzle from them subtly, cautiously.

Until she had the answer, or a portion of it, at least.

No one she spoke to seemed to know the Iceman, although several of them knew his name and reputation. Some warned her to forget about him, and one, at last, had given up a Pasadena address.

"It's a high-rent playhouse," she was told. "The dude you're looking for runs all his major action out of there."

And Cherry did not need to hear precisely what that "action" might consist of. She had picked up rumbles on the street already, running down the Iceman's varied interests. Everything from kiddie porn to rumors of a snuff-film racket, and while she knew enough to take the street talk with a grain of salt, it was becoming obvious that Frank LaMancha's target was one heavy operator.

She had waited for the soldier's call until her patience was exhausted. Cherry realized he might not get in touch with her again; there would be nothing to prevent him going on about his private quest and leaving her behind. He owed her nothing, after all, had never even touched her. But she still felt a bond between them that prevented her from letting go and lighting out for parts unknown without a last attempt to get in touch.

LaMancha owed her nothing.

But she owed something to the hardman, and she meant to pay him back no matter what the risks involved.

He had restored a measure of her self-respect, her pride—if that was possible—and Cherry Gifford owed the man for that. And he had taught her that survival was not necessarily the top priority. It was the quality of life, not mere existence, that determined human worth. Not only staying hard, but something else that he called *living large*.

The lady was not sure if she was capable of living up to Frank LaMancha's standard, but she knew damned well that she had never lived so large as when they had fought together in Hotel Hell. She had been fighting for her life, not bargaining her soul away for mere survival of the body, and the feelings it evoked inside her were re-juvenating.

And so, yes, she owed a debt to Frank LaMancha. One that she was almost eager to repay.

When she could wait no longer, Cherry Gifford dug inside her handbag, found the number that LaMancha had provided, scribbled on a matchbook. He would not be there—she knew that much—but he had left the number with her "just in case," explaining that whoever answered would be able to communicate with him in an emergency.

Like now.

Her hands were trembling as she dialed, and Cherry chalked up two wrong numbers before she finally got it right. She waited through four rings, was finally answered by a soft male voice, and she used the password that LaMancha had given her.

"Let me talk to Lazarus."

"He's out right now," the soft voice said, and it had taken on a sudden edge. "If there's a message. . ."

She thought about it for a moment, listening to airy silence on the line, and then she laid it out as simply and concisely as she could.

"I've found the guy he's looking for," she told her faceless contact, "out in Pasadena."

"Have you got an address?"

Cherry rattled off the numbers, listened and confirmed the message as he read them back to her correctly.

"Will he get that right away?"

A cautious note behind the other voice. "As soon as he checks in, I'll pass the word."

"How long has he been out of touch?" she asked, an icy prickle spreading across her scalp.

More hesitation on the other end.

"It's been a while."

Goddammit!

If there had been trouble, if he had been hurt somehow—or even killed—then it was over, done before it really started.

Unless she carried on what he had begun and worked with what she knew to give herself a leg up on the opposition.

"Listen, if he calls—"

"Yes?"

Cherry hesitated briefly, finally made her mind up. "Nothing. Never mind."

"Hey, wait a sec—"

She cradled the receiver, cutting off the other voice in midsyllable. He was about to warn her off, she knew, advise her to stay clear and let the big boys play among themselves.

Except it wouldn't wash. Not anymore.

She had already played a hand or two herself, and she was well aware of what comprised the table stakes.

This game was life-and-death, and she had already managed to survive the preliminary rounds. Now the lady felt that she was ready for the finals. It would have been more comforting to make the game a doubles match with Frank LaMancha at her side, but she would have to settle for a round of solitaire this time.

It would be a long cab ride to Pasadena, but the soldier had endowed her handsomely.

Chief among her problems would be exactly what to do when she arrived at her destination. She could not waltz into the Iceman's high-rent playhouse and simply announce herself, that was certain. Neither could she risk appearing too inquisitive about the man himself. . . not if she wanted to come out again in one piece. It had to be a casual move, entirely *natural*. . . .

After almost half an hour, Cherry Gifford felt that she had come to the solution of her problem. There were risks involved, of course, but she would have a fighting chance to get inside the playhouse, anyway, and once inside. . .

Enough for now.

She glanced around the little room, made certain she was leaving nothing behind before she snapped her handbag shut and moved in the direction of the door. She hesitated, almost left a note, and then decided that LaMancha was more likely to be checking with his service than returning here to read a scribbled message.

If he checked in with his contact, he would get the word.

If he came looking for her, he would know where she had gone.

If he was still alive.

18

Captain Tim Braddock drew a thick black *X* through yesterday and pushed the desk-top calendar away from him, cursing softly under his breath.

Twelve days. . .and with the time off he had coming, it was only ten days on the streets.

He cursed again, more loudly this time.

He could damn well say goodbye to those days off, the captain knew from long experience. With all the sudden action they were having, he'd be lucky if he did not draw a double shift straight through to the retirement ceremony.

Dammit!

What he did not need right now was something that had taken on the earmarks of a full-blown gang war. All that butcher's work at Hotel Hell was bad enough, but now someone was knocking over hot spots tended by the syndicate, even barging in on a celebrity or two at home. It was the kind of thing he had not seen since. . .

Braddock stopped himself before he could complete the thought, his fingers toying absentmindedly with something on his desk. He picked it up and turned it over in his hands, allowing it to catch the pale fluorescent light. And for just an instant it seemed to shine with some faint inner light, as if it might have come alive, been winking at him about secret knowledge that they shared.

He dropped the marksman's medal in a pocket, reconsidered, finally shut it inside his top desk drawer.

This was the last thing he needed on the verge of his retirement, and Braddock clung tenaciously to hopes that he was wrong, that mere coincidence would finally explain it all away.

He had retrieved the marksman's medal from a "film producer" known—but never prosecuted—for his drug connections. By the time the homicide captain talked to him, the guy was stone-sober, well beyond the reach of any tranquilizer in his agitation. Braddock smelled the fear as the producer poured his story out, and there was no point in denying it.

He liked the smell.

It pleased him that someone, somehow, had finally shaken up this pompous bastard to the point where he was trembling for his worthless life and whining for police protection. He would get it, naturally, for money talked around L.A., as elsewhere. Still . . .

Tim Braddock had not felt such downright satisfaction watching someone squirm since . . .

Hell, admit it.

Since Mack Bolan's visit to Los Angeles.

There.

His pulse had skipped a beat when he first saw the marksman's medal, heard the "victim" sketch a vague description of his adversary and the military gear he carried . . . but with time, the veteran of Homicide had managed to convince himself that he was jumping to conclusions.

Well, almost.

There was the medal coupled with the fact that none of his informers on the street knew anything about a beef within the L.A. Family that might account for all the sudden mayhem. That much, and continuing reports from all along the Eastern Seaboard that his man was very much alive and kicking ass the way he used to.

But even granting that the stories might be true did not put the Executioner in Braddock's jurisdiction. There was a world of targets out there waiting for him, all deserving, and it was too much to think that lightning would strike twice in Braddock's own backyard.

And yet . . .

The jangling of the telephone beside his elbow took Tim Braddock by surprise. It almost made him jump, and then the big cop grinned at his reaction and lifted the receiver to his ear.

"Homicide. Braddock."

There was a moment's hesitation on the other end, and then the voice came through.

"It's been a long time, Captain."

Braddock stiffened in his desk chair, conscious of the gooseflesh rising on his arms. It felt like something from the stories told to children, how you knew it, felt it, when somebody walked across your grave.

And it had been a long time, sure, but there was no denying that Tim Braddock recognized the voice.

Mack Bolan's voice.

"I hope this call's long-distance," Braddock told the stony warrior, willing rigid muscles to relax as he sank back into his chair.

"It's strictly local," Bolan answered, and his words confirmed the half fears that had haunted Braddock since the night before at Hotel Hell.

"Okay. I guess that answers damn near all the questions I've been asking for the past twelve hours."

There was no instant answer on the other end, and Braddock forged ahead.

"You've been a busy boy."

"It's not done yet."

An arctic chill ran down his spine, demanding an involuntary tremor from the big detective.

"That right?"

"I'm after Bobby Benedetto," Bolan told him candidly. "When he's gone, so am I."

"Why Benedetto?" Braddock asked impulsively. "You settling for number two these days?"

"He's number one in my book," Bolan answered. "Andriola doesn't cut it anymore."

"He'll be surprised to hear that, guy."

"I'm betting Bobby finds a way to pass the message sooner than you might expect."

"Oh, yeah?"

The man from Homicide was listening intently now, and wondering how far to trust the Executioner's information. As soon as he had formed the question, though, Braddock passed it off. He knew the answer in his mind and heart already.

He trusted Bolan's intel all the way.

"So why tell me?"

"There's more at stake than just a simple hit-and-run," the soldier said. "I may need help."

It was a startling admission from the Executioner, and all the more so when the captain thought of what it must have taken for him to pronounce the words in conversation with a cop.

I may need help.

Braddock felt a churning in his gut, a sudden throbbing ache behind his eyes. It was, he thought, not so unlike the first time he looked down the muzzle of a hostile gun and knew that it was do or die right now, no time for second thoughts.

"I'm listening," he said.

And Bolan spelled it out for him in graphic detail. Foster Price. The daughter. Blackmail. Bobby Benedetto and his stinking empire.

Snuff films, right.

When he had finished speaking, Braddock sat in silence for a moment, mulling over possibilities inside his head. There were alternatives, of course. He could refuse the offer of cooperation outright, going strictly by the book. Or he could try to sucker Bolan, draw him into range with bullshit promises before he sprang the trap—and sent himself into retirement with a king-size feather in his cap.

The captain scowled. Make that a goddamned albatross around his neck if he betrayed this confidence. No matter what was written in the book, a soldier—or a lawman—had to do some thinking for himself along the way.

And that brought Captain Braddock to the third alternative.

"What do you need?" he asked.

Another moment passed with Bolan doing all the talking, Braddock taking mental notes. It sounded simple on its face, and yet the big cop knew that if he muffed it, he could kiss those thirty years goodbye, his pension—hell, his freedom. If anyone caught on to what he had in mind...

"I understand," he said when Bolan finished. There was still a chance to slam the door and lock it tight, but he had tried that route before and learned that it kept nothing out. "I'll see what I can do."

It was Mack Bolan's turn to hesitate, to search for words. He settled for, "I owe you one."

Tim Braddock smiled. "Let's call it even, soldier."

"Fair enough. And thanks."

The line went cold, and Braddock cradled the receiver softly, rocking back and staring at the telephone for several moments in reflective silence. He was lining up the bits and pieces in his mind, already thinking through the problems that would lie ahead of him if he went through with Bolan's plan.

No. Scratch that "if."

He was committed, and he would go through with it. If not for Bolan's sake, then for his own.

And it was time to move. He would need every moment that he had to put it all together for their rendezvous. No point in thinking about what would happen after, when it all was done. There might not be an "after," but it didn't seem to matter anymore.

Tim Braddock rose and moved around his desk, already reaching for the coatrack when a tiny shard of memory fell into place. He circled back, retrieved the marksman's medal from his desk drawer and thrust it deep inside a pocket of his slacks.

All right, so let it rip. There would be no regrets or second thoughts about this choice. Not this time. He had played the first round from the book. This time around he would be following the heart and going by some old rules that were sometimes overlooked in modern manuals on police procedure.

Rules like justice. Like right and wrong.

And while they might be out of fashion at the moment, they were far from obsolete. Tonight they just might jog some memories in that regard. If so it would be worth the risk. If not. . .

Well, it might be worth it anyway.

THE CALL TO CAPTAIN BRADDOCK was a gamble, Bolan knew, but for the moment it appeared to have paid off. If Bolan read the Homicide detective right, his contribution to the final phase of Bolan's Hollywood campaign might be a crucial one.

The Executioner had crossed Tim Braddock's path before, and they had been on opposite sides that time, the cop committed to arresting Bolan or to killing him. It had been nothing personal—on Bolan's end, at any rate. He had realized that Braddock had a job to do and would not have respected him if he had tried to do it less than thoroughly. He had acquired a feeling for the captain when they tangled, more so when Carl Lyons, Braddock's second-in-command, came over to the Bolan team fulltime. And there was something. . .

Braddock struck him as committed, right, but to ideals,

not just to the concept of a job. He was the kind of officer—the kind of soldier—who might bend a rule or two to reach his goal, providing he believed implicitly that he was right.

There was the possibility, of course, that he might play along with Bolan on the telephone and have an army waiting to corral him when they met, but Bolan knew he would have to take that chance. It was an ever-present risk in these hellgrounds; he had faced it often, and he would not let the risk deter him from his course.

The Executioner had set some goals himself, and he would reach them or expend his life in the attempt. If Braddock helped him, fine. If not... well, he would do his utmost to avoid a shooting confrontation with the men in uniform. Thus far, he had not fired on any soldiers of the same side in his private war, and he did not intend to alter his procedures now.

Once you started compromising, you ran the risk of waking up one morning and discovering your enemy reflected in the bathroom mirror. And once that line was crossed, once you had joined the savages in spirit, there could be no turning back.

As for Mack Bolan, his determined course lay straight ahead. He was following the one-way signposts, sure, until he reached the end of the line.

In Hollywood the signposts led to Bobby Benedetto, alias the Iceman, and the Executioner had done some double-checking on his facts before he placed the call to Homicide. He knew that Benedetto's Pasadena joint, Club Venus, was regarded as the home away from home for many of the L.A. area's most influential citizens. Attorneys, politicians, businessmen—and women—went there to relax, to shed their inhibitions, to rub shoulders with the denizens of those gray zones on the outskirts of the law. It was a private club, of course, and what went on within the ivy-covered walls remained inside...unless the owner, say, decided that some mention of it might pay off for him.

Bolan knew the sort of place, and he knew there was no way on God's earth the courts would ever get around to putting padlocks on the doors, no matter who might be abused or used inside. The membership of Bobby Benedetto's private club had pull, that all-important asset in a town where money talked.

But if the cops and courts were powerless to close Club Venus, that posed no obstacle to a determined Executioner. He had no need for warrants or injunctions, and there would be no appealing his decisions once the sentence had been handed down.

And judgment day was coming for the Iceman, for Club Venus, for whoever sided with the animals in raping and degrading women, children...anyone they could afford to buy. The cleansing fire was drawing closer by the moment, and tonight there would be heat enough to go around, damn right.

If Braddock held his end up, the survivors just might have a chance to tell their side in court, attempt to sell their lifestyle to a jury of their peers. And if the Homicide detective changed his mind...

Well, then, the high-class savages would have to take their chances side by side with Bobby Benedetto and his sewer rats. A bullet did not take the time to check a target out for average yearly income or the latest in designer clothes.

Mack Bolan would prefer a surgical incision to a massacre, but he could play it either way, depending on exactly how the cards were dealt. If Braddock played it straight, with no surprise ace hidden up his sleeve....

Braddock would come through—or he would not—and either way, Mack Bolan's mission was the same. To strike a telling blow against the cannibals. To cut down as many of them as he could in his allotted time onstage, and if he had to exit prematurely, to make sure that some of them accompanied him.

The soldier had been traveling along Blood River long enough to know that no man has a guarantee on tomorrow. Every hour is a lifetime, to be used or wasted, with a tab presented at the point of debarkation. And Mack Bolan was convinced that, come his private judgment day, the universe would not be searching him for medals, but for scars. The symbols of an active *doing* life, damn right.

His chosen course would justify—or condemn—itself, and there was no point now in trying to outguess the future.

There were plans to lay and final preparations to be made before he faced the dragon in its den. No warrior lived as long as Bolan had without attending carefully to all the details that came before a battle. No soldier lived to fight another day unless he made some bare provisions for the day to come.

The plan he had in mind was fairly simple: he was going into Bobby Benedetto's club, sans invitation, to exterminate the landlord and to extricate one special and involuntary guest. If Julie Price was not on site, it would be Bolan's task to keep the Iceman, and himself, alive until he learned her whereabouts.

He had no way to gauge the level of security that Benedetto might employ around Club Venus. Long years of protection from officials might have softened Bobby somewhat, but Bolan was not ready yet to stake his life on supposition.

He was going hard, damn right, and when, inevitably, Benedetto's muscle tried to stop him, well . . .

The night would no doubt harbor some surprises, yeah, for all concerned.

The wild-card factor could not be avoided in a case like this, where no time was allotted for in-depth reconnaissance. Delay on this one might prove fatal—for the plan, for Julie Price—and Bolan would prefer to face the risks involved when his only alternative was to watch everything that he had worked for slip between his fingers.

The soldier finished sorting his gear, then tried another call to Cherry Gifford, one more time with brother John... and came up empty, two-for-two. He was concerned but not yet worried as he set down the receiver after his final try and turned back to the job of double-checking weaponry.

His brother was a grown man now, a battle-tested veteran. As for Cherry...

His frown became a scowl, and Bolan forced her from his mind now, concentrating on the task at hand with singleness of purpose.

Later...if there was a later...he would have the time to wonder what had happened to her, even look for her if he was so inclined.

Right now, the warrior had a war to fight. Julie Price. Club Venus. The Iceman. All demanded his attention, and he could not well afford distractions on the eve of mortal combat.

Mack Bolan was about to face an army, and the fate of one lone street child could not take priority. Except that Cherry counted, right.

But she would have to wait until he met the dragon one-on-one, until the issue was decided.

19

The girl sat up in bed, supported by her outstretched arms, and waited for the sudden dizziness to fade. It seemed the drugs were getting weaker . . . or perhaps she was developing a tolerance. Either way, it was a start.

She could recall her name, her family, and while the date eluded her, at least she had a grasp of where she was. Not the address, but she could recognize the kind of place.

And Julie Price was well aware that she was in deep trouble.

The radio had roused her, and she focused her attention on it now, concentrating on the sound and praying for her head to clear. The dial was set on FM, and Bonnie Tyler was holding out for a hero till the end of the night, her sharp voice cutting through the fog that hovered over Julie's consciousness.

She shook her head, debated whether she should try to stand, and put it off another moment. There was too much rubber in her legs right now, and she would never make it to the bathroom, let alone the outside hallway and beyond . . . the lawn . . . the gate. . . .

It was a foolish mind game, anyway, she knew. The bedroom door was locked as always, and she was not going anywhere until the Iceman or one of her attendants came to get her for the next performance.

Julie hung her head and let the scalding tears run freely down her cheeks. She did not have to ask how she had come to this; the drugs had not deprived her of her memory to the extent that she could not recall the past few months, the parties that seemed to last forever, and, in time, the films.

It had not been so bad when she was starting out. No different, really, than the parties where she let herself be passed around from hand to hand, enjoying it—almost—because she knew that it would hurt her father if he knew. She did not hate him, when she got right down to cases, but she felt neglected since her mother's death...deserted for the law and politics and everything that took him away from her.

And somewhere she had crossed the line, until she woke up one morning, stoned, and found that she was virtually a prisoner.

While she did not know precisely what the Iceman might have going for himself, it figured that her father was involved, the Senate race...whatever.

Julie guessed that she had finally found a way to hurt him, to get his full attention for the first time. And all that it had cost her was her dignity, her freedom, and very possibly, she thought, her life.

There was no clock inside the bedroom, but a glance through windows fitted with "decorative" prison bars informed her that the sun was going down.

They would be coming for her soon, and in the meantime there was nothing she could do about it.

Mere captivity would not have been so bad, she thought, although the idea would have sickened her at one time. It was the rest of it—the old men with their slicked-down hair and manicured nails; the four- and five-man "parties" where she was expected to play "hostess" while the Iceman cranked his cameras up behind the scenes—that made her sometimes wish the drugs were stronger. Strong enough to wipe out all sensation, perhaps to wipe out life itself.

Suicidal thoughts were frequent now, and they no longer shocked or terrified her as they once had. If this was living—

On the radio the singer brought her song to an explosive

climax, wailing for a white knight who would carry her away to... what? No matter, really. Anything would have to be a great improvement on the present.

She could use a hero of her own right now, the lady thought. Damn right. No need for armor, necessarily. Just pick the lock—or smash it, sure—and have a fast car waiting at the gate. No sweat.

But what about the Iceman?

Julie knew that he would never let her go as long as there was any way that he could use her for his own advancement, even to satisfy a whim. His cruelty was almost legendary on the streets among the runaways and would-be actresses who ended up in sleazy porn films.

The guy was sick, no doubt about it. Warped in ways that her imagination could not have conceived. She had encountered freaks who got their thrills from hurting or from being hurt, but this one was another story altogether.

But no one was doing anything about the Iceman, and no one ever would. This ghoul was sheltered by the wealthy perverts he serviced; they protected him and nurtured his malignancy, preferring not to recognize the evidence before their eyes so long as he, in turn, provided what they craved. And if he got a bit too rough with this or that rejected runaway, well, Hollywood was teeming with them, after all.

She heard her captors coming well before they reached her bedroom door. The drugs, somehow, had intensified her senses even as they robbed her of the will to form coherent thought, the sheer initiative to act. She heard their footsteps, and then the key turned softly, opening the latch that held her prisoner.

The Iceman filled her doorway, tall, broad shouldered, muscular. She thought, not for the first time, that he must have been good-looking once—might still be to a woman who was unaware of what went on behind the slate-gray eyes. When Julie looked at him these days, she saw beneath the sunlamp tan, the perfect haircut, to the death mask that personified his evil.

In the hallway, hanging back behind his master, Julie recognized the strong-arm guard she knew as Mario. He was a bastard in his own right, but the Iceman was her problem now, and she concentrated on avoiding contact with his eyes.

"So, how's it going, Julie?"

"All right," she answered listlessly, pretending to be more drugged than she felt.

She felt his smile like a caress from filthy hands.

"That's good. You need your rest, babe. I've got something special for you later on this evening."

Julie made no answer, but she raised her eyes to face him for the first time since he'd entered. He was staring at her pointedly, with the expression of a starving man who had encountered an unexpected feast. The glimmer in his eyes provoked involuntary shudders, and she saw him smile, a death's-head grimace.

"Something special, babe," he said again. "You're gonna love it."

She felt her stomach turning over, and was thankful that she had not eaten now in...what? Would it be hours? Days? She kept her face impassive as he winked at her and turned away, brushed past Mario and let his flunky lock the door.

Alone again, she lay back on the bed, her hands clenched into tiny fists against her sides. She did not need to think about what "something special" might mean to the Iceman. There was no point in attempting to anticipate what new abuse—or variation of an old one—might have taken shape inside his twisted mind. She would find out the details soon enough.

Too soon.

And it was too damned bad that all the heroes were confined to songs these days. Too bad, indeed.

She brushed away the first few tears and finally gave it up as hopeless. Maybe, with a little luck, she just might cry herself to sleep and get some rest before the Iceman came for her again. And maybe, with a lot of luck, she might never wake up.

A DRIVEBY TOLD JOHNNY BOLAN everything that he could learn about Club Venus from the outside. He circled once around the block before he pulled his sports car onto the driveway, rolling to a halt before the massive wrought-iron gates. A moment, then they rumbled open far enough to let a gate man, uniformed and armed, approach the car.

It was a gamble, but there seemed no other way to go. If he was able to get by on nerve, employing information he had gained from some preliminary phone calls to selected friends, then he would be inside.

He wound down the driver's window, flashed the uniform a friendly smile.

"How goes it?"

"May I help you, sir?"

He recognized the tone. Efficient, quasi-military. And the guy would play it by the book, right down the line. With any luck, it just might be the edge that Johnny Bolan needed.

"I'm late," he said, as if it should have told the gate man everything.

"How's that, sir?"

"I was s'posed to meet the judge at his place and we'd all come out together," Johnny told him, keeping up the smile. "I got hung up awhile, but here I am."

An eyebrow undulated, not quite rising.

"What judge would that be, sir?"

The guard's eyes flickered recognition of the name, and he stepped back to scan the single sheet of paper on a clipboard that he carried. Halfway down the page his index finger traced a name, then he leaned forward toward the car.

"The judge is here," he said. "But I'm afraid he didn't leave us any word that you were coming."

"What?" Johnny feigned amazement. "Well, now, what the hell. *Dammit!*"

Johnny felt the gate man watching him, and knew that he could not afford to overplay his hand. He glanced around for some sign of a telephone or walkie-talkie.

"Is there some way you could call and have him paged? I know he'll clear this up if I can have a word with him."

The guard glanced back in the direction of the house, attempting to make up his mind. It seemed as though he stood there a lifetime before he straightened up, put both hands on his hips, the clipboard tucked beneath one arm.

"I guess you might as well go on ahead," he said, and smiled. "No sense in interrupting the judge."

Johnny beamed, fishing down in his pocket, withdrawing a sawbuck and handing it over. "Hey, thanks. You're a lifesaver."

"Sure. And thank *you*, sir. Enjoy."

"Oh, I plan to," Johnny told the man's retreating back.

He waited for the double gates to open wide, then drove on through, a final parting wave in the direction of the uniform before he powered on along the curving gravel drive. He pulled the sportster up in front of a palatial manor house and climbed out as a liveried valet moved down the steps to greet him. Grudgingly, he let go of the car keys, watching as the guy picked out a space some fifty yards away.

Not far, but it could damn well feel like fifty miles if he was under fire and running for his life. He shrugged the thought away, deciding that he had no options now that he had come this far, and went inside.

The crowded foyer of Club Venus looked like something from the 1890s, with its crystal chandeliers and hanging tapestries.

A butler met him in the entryway, but Johnny waved

him off, declining to give up the jacket that concealed his hardware. Beneath one arm, a semiautomatic KG-99 hung muzzle down in shoulder rigging, and the sport coat had been cut a half size larger to help disguise it. Special pockets sewn into the lining held three box magazines, a total of 108 9mm parabellum rounds.

Enough spare ammunition to cover everybody in the mansion, if it came to that. But Johnny Bolan had come looking for a lady, not a massacre.

It was no more than a long shot, Johnny knew, to cherish hopes of finding her alone without some kind of guard on duty. They would keep a close watch on her if they knew what they were doing...and from all appearances, the manor house had not been built on ignorance.

It was a rich man's playground, prepared to cope with any whim a paying customer might have. The girls he saw downstairs were technically still dressed, but their attire left very little to the imagination, and the couples clenching here and there around the large main room were clearly undeterred by any sense of modesty. He guessed that as the night went on, as liquor flowed and lines of coke were sucked up into greedy nostrils from the special glass-topped coffee tables, inhibitions would be dropped along with trousers and the guests would settle back to let the good times roll.

He did not plan to wait around that long, however. The success of his mission hinged on timing. Once he found the girl—if she was here at all—he would be living on the numbers. One slip and he could kiss it all goodbye.

A glance around the crowded room turned up a face or two that Johnny recognized, and one or two that raised the young man's eyebrows. Still, he had not come here to judge a group of wealthy swingers. There was nothing downstairs, and he finally concluded that the guest in search of "specialties" would find them somewhere else, perhaps upstairs.

It was a shot, and he began to work his way across the room, encountering resistance on the way from some determined lovelies who were bent on getting friendly with the new arrival. Johnny disengaged himself before their hands could come in contact with the KG-99.

Two or three men passed on the stairs, all coming down, and he met no challenge on the way. The friendly ladies were forgotten now as he approached the landing on the second floor and found a corridor leading off to either side. He counted twenty doors to bedrooms or whatever, finally giving up and wondering if he would have to check them all. If so, he might be there all night and on into the dawn without success.

A footfall on the stairs behind him startled Johnny, brought him right around to find himself confronted by a tall man wearing a tuxedo, which appeared to be the standard uniform for the help around Club Venus. This one might have been the bouncer, based upon his size and the way he moved. He was eyeing Johnny with frank suspicion tempered by a trace of artificial courtesy.

"Yes, sir? There something I can do for you?"

"I hope so, friend. I'm looking for the can, and if it ain't close by, we're gonna need some waders here."

The bouncer flashed a mirthless grin, then something flickered behind the dark, unsmiling eyes. He cocked a thumb across one shoulder, pointed back along the stairs, and slipped the single button on his jacket simultaneously with his free hand, acting casual. The jacket gapped, providing him with easy access to whatever lay beneath it.

"Back downstairs," he said. "You missed it, partner."

Johnny thanked him, stepped off toward the stairs, and instantly whipped back around, his left hand flashing out to pin the bouncer's gun arm at his side, the right already bunched into a fist when it impacted with the guy's nose. A fan of scarlet sprayed across the ruffled shirt and stained the dark tuxedo jacket.

Johnny heard the numbers running now, and none of them were wasted as he followed through with yet another hard right to the solar plexus, doubling his opposition over, priming him to eat a rising knee that flipped him on his back. A glance downstairs revealed that they had not been noticed, and he quickly dragged the goon toward some privacy.

The first door Johnny tried swung open, and they were through it in an instant. He draped the groggy thug across the king-size bed and reached inside the man's tuxedo jacket. He found an autoloading pistol and slid it from its belly holster into his belt before he set about reviving the gorilla.

The bouncer would have some idea of what was going on inside Club Venus, who was here at any given time and whether they were under guard. He would impart that knowledge, given adequate incentive, and a quest that might have lasted hours would be cut to minutes.

Providing that she had not been moved.

Providing that she had ever seen the inside of Club Venus in the first place.

It was still a long shot, right . . . but he had known that going in. And it was still the only shot he had, the only chance to help his brother out of what had turned into a major shooting war across Los Angeles.

20

The *capo* of Los Angeles was slowly starting to relax. It had been several hours now since he'd received reports of any action on the streets. It seemed that Bobby Benedetto might have done his job successfully. The kid had talent, Vinnie Andriola had to give him that, and if he bagged the renegade, well, it might be worth a bonus.

Vincent Andriola could afford some generosity. From all appearances he had survived another shooting war, and while he still had no firm handle on precisely who or why he had been fighting, that could wait till later. Benedetto would be calling shortly to report his progress.

And if the renegade turned out to be Mack Bolan, as he had feared from the appearance of the dreaded marksman's medals, then there would be ample cause for celebration in the Andriola household. Bolan's head could be his ticket to the top, a guaranteed commission seat, for openers. If he bagged the Executioner...

Reality snapped back at him like ice-cold water dumped into his lap.

And if he did not have the Bolan scalp to hang among his other trophies—then what?

Suppose the renegade was only that, some psycho on a rampage or a cop gone off the deep end to extract some justice of his own. There would be nothing but embarrassment for Andriola if a crackpot with an ax to grind could hold his Family at bay and dish out so much punishment before they brought him down. Instead of gaining new prestige he would be in for rank humiliation by the other *capos*, who were bound to see the episode as a sign of weakness.

There was a chance, of course, that all his troubles were the natural result of an incursion by some other Family attempting to feel out his strength before they launched a major strike. They would have been encouraged, Andriola knew, by the initial chaos in his ranks, but there was still a chance that he could hold his own.

If Bobby Benedetto did his job.

The jangling extension phone surprised him, but he let the houseman take it, hoping it was nothing that demanded his attention. He was irritated when the knock came on his study door.

"Come in."

The houseman poked his head inside. "Some joker wants to talk to you, sir, and he won't take no. He said it has to do with Mr. Benedetto, and you'll want to hear him out."

The *capo*'s frown became a scowl. "All right. I've got it."

The door was closing as he lifted the receiver, making certain not to hide his irritation.

"So, let's have it."

"Vinnie? Hey, it's good to hear your voice."

"I don't think we been introduced."

The smart-ass pushed ahead, ignoring him.

"I thought I might already be too late, you know? Like, maybe I'd be talking to the coroner or something by the time your housecock put me on."

"You want a conversation," Andriola cautioned, "I'd suggest you start making some sense."

"Hey, Vinnie, don't get tense, okay? So, Bobby's late. That only means you've got more time to lay the welcome mat."

"I'm tired of this," the mafioso growled.

"You tired of living, too?"

"If there's a point to this, you better make it."

"It's made already, man. Your number two has put it all together for himself."

"You're talking shit."

"Could be. But there's a solid rumble on the street that you're the asshole getting wiped tonight."

A chill had settled at the base of Vinnie Andriola's skull, and it was spreading out now, icy fingers tickling his scalp beneath the thinning hair.

"I'm listening. But cut the runaround, okay?"

"Fair enough. I thought you might be interested in knowing Benedetto's going for himself. I thought it might be worth a little something."

"Sure. Providing that you've got it straight."

"It's straight, okay. He's mobbing up right now, out at his cathouse, Venus whatchacallit, getting set to pay you all a visit."

Something clicked in Andriola's head, the sound of final pieces falling into place.

"If this is true—"

"Why don't you check it out, you don't believe me?"

"Maybe I'll just do that, mister. . ."

"No names, hey? You find the information's useful, I'll be back in touch when everything gets sorted out all peaceful like."

"If this is straight, it won't take long."

"Just watch yourself, okay? I don't like backing losers."

And the line went dead, the dial tone humming in his ear obnoxiously until he hung up the receiver with an angry gesture. Smart-ass bastard! Who the hell did he think—

Andriola stopped himself, concentrating on the problem of the moment. If the caller had been playing straight with him—and why the hell would some damned stranger call his private number just to play a farfetched joke?—then he was looking at the explanation of his troubles all wrapped up in one tight package.

Bobby Benedetto moving on his own, and sure, why not? He was ambitious, hungry, capable.

More capable, perhaps, than Andriola was himself.

The *capo* of Los Angeles dismissed the thought, intent on getting to the bottom of this riddle without delay. If Benedetto was around Club Venus, with his troops or otherwise, it was a simple matter to check out. And if the check proved positive. . . .

The mafioso planned to make this field inspection personally, with enough hard guns behind him to take care of any challenge he might meet along the way. If Bobby "Two-Faced" Benedetto thought he could put something over on his own damned boss, then he had a lesson coming to him that would take his breath away.

MACK BOLAN MADE THE SIX-FOOT DROP and landed in shadow just inside the decorative wall that screened Club Venus from the outside world. He froze, a living statue in the darkness, every combat sense alert to warning signals of impending danger. . . and he came up empty.

Bolan was in blacksuit, hands and face discolored with cosmetic camouflage. Big Thunder, the .44 AutoMag, rode his hip on military webbing, and the Beretta 93-R was in place beneath his arm. The Uzi submachine gun slung across his chest was Bolan's front-line weapon for the probe, its 750-round-per-minute cyclic rate entirely adequate for any opposition he expected to encounter in the Iceman's love nest. Extra magazines, grenades, a K-bar fighting knife and strangling gear were carried on the military harness that he wore, with other extras tucked away inside the hidden pockets of his skinsuit.

Finally certain that he was indeed alone, the Executioner moved in the direction of the manor house. He purposely avoided contact with the driveway, keeping to the wooded grounds. In moments he reached the edge of the trees, peering out from cover of shadows, examining the house that was his final destination.

It would be early yet for Captain Braddock to arrive, providing that the Homicide detective kept their bargain. Vinnie Andriola was another problem, though, and if he took the bait, he could be arriving with his soldiers anytime.

Calling Andriola was a calculated risk, the soldier realized, but one that he could not have avoided. He did not plan on wiping Bobby Benedetto, taking out one man or one regime, while all the rotten rest of it remained intact. The Iceman was his target, right, but Benedetto was just a symptom of the general malignancy that he had diagnosed in Hollywood. A Mafia malignancy, for sure, but with its scabrous tendrils reaching out to foul society at large.

And worst of all, society had made the creeping cancer welcome.

If there were any innocents inside Club Venus, they had been abducted, drugged, recruited through coercion, deception by the Iceman's chicken hawks. The patrons who arrived in limousines to wile away their time inside the serpent's nest were every bit as rotten—more so, maybe—than Bolan's quarry of the moment.

The Executioner had faith that Captain Braddock would be able to take care of them: the businessmen and politicians, judges, pillars of "polite society." There would be no convictions, almost certainly, no jail time. Even fines would be unlikely under the circumstances. But there might be other ways: a tip to newsmen just before the raid; a long march underneath the floodlights past the rolling cameras.

Film at eleven, damn right, and you could tuck your reputation up there with the family honor where the moon would never shine. Kiss off those man- or lady-of-the-year awards this time around, for sure, and make a stab at running down an explanation for the wife or husband, for the kids, for all those "friends" who would be whispering your name around the country club.

It was a start.

And then there was the Iceman, primed and ready for a special dose of jungle justice that would melt him down to nothing but a rancid memory.

The Executioner pushed off from cover, sprinting over open ground to the direction of the house.

His quarry had been waiting long enough.

"I'LL ASK IT ONE TIME. Have you seen her?"

The gorilla used his hand to wipe blood from his nostrils, glaring at the photograph of Julie Price in Johnny Bolan's hand.

"Hey, man—"

He shut up as the young man raised his captured autoloader, thumbing back the hammer, muzzle inches from his face.

"One chance. Don't waste it."

"You use that thing in here, you'll have an army on your ass."

"Well, one thing's sure," his captor told him earnestly. "You won't be here to watch."

The bouncer thought about it for a moment, finally nodding in agreement with the Bolan logic.

"Yeah, all right, just take it easy, huh? She's one floor up. End of the hall, on your left."

The pistol came to rest against his forehead, grafted to the sweaty flesh.

"I hope you're smart enough to play it straight," Johnny Bolan said.

And the gorilla risked a shaky smile. "Why would I lie? You'll never make it ten feet with her anyway. This place is covered, man, you dig?"

"I dig."

He brought the pistol back just far enough to give himself momentum when he cracked it against the bouncer's skull. The pistolero slumped over on the mattress, all the fight gone out of him at once.

If the bouncer had been smart or scared enough to tell the truth, then Johnny had a solid fix on Julie Price. With any luck, she might not have a standing guard to keep her company. His job might be a cakewalk.

And maybe on his way upstairs he'd find somebody who was interested in purchasing the Brooklyn Bridge.

Johnny grinned.

The odds of finding Julie Price and extricating her without encountering the opposition would be slim enough, he knew. The odds of exiting Club Venus unopposed were something else again.

Like astronomical.

He slipped the autoloader inside the waistband of his slacks and brought the KG-99 from underneath his jacket, hefting it in one hand. It was short, a bare 12.5 inches, but the flat black finish and its vented barrel shrouding gave the piece an awesome look.

Johnny snapped a long box magazine in place and drew the bolt back, chambered up the first of thirty-six 9mm parabellum rounds. A gentle pressure on the operating handle set the safety, and he slid the weapon back beneath his jacket, suspended from its harness, ready at his need.

It made a bulky outline with the magazine in place, but Johnny was not going to a fashion show. And anyone he met from here on in would more than likely be an enemy.

He double-checked the bouncer, satisfied himself that there would be no danger from that quarter for a while, and moved out. The hallway was deserted, and he back-tracked toward the stairs, encountering no opposition on his short climb to the floor above.

And this floor, like the one below, seemed to be deserted. That was fine with Johnny, but he kept the buttons of his jacket undone just the same, his KG-99 and the gorilla's captured pistol easily within his reach.

"End of the hall. On your left," the thug had told him.

He stood before the door and silently tested the knob. Locked. No point in knocking, Johnny reasoned; if there was a prisoner inside the room, she would be under guard or somehow unable to release the lock from her side of the door. In either case it would be useless—and quite likely fatal—to announce his presence prematurely.

One more glance along the corridor and Johnny brought the semiautomatic KG-99 from beneath his coat. He snapped the safety off, stepped back and drove his heel with stunning force against the door.

The locking mechanism shattered, and Johnny was inside within a heartbeat, his eyes and weapon sweeping the room, finding no one but the lady sitting upright in the middle of the bed.

And even now, light-years away from smiling high-school photographs, he had no problem recognizing Julie Price.

Her eyes were fastened on the gun as Johnny closed the bedroom door behind him and swiftly crossed to give the tiny bathroom cubicle a cautionary glance. When he was satisfied that they were alone, he lowered the weapon, letting it hang against his side.

"Who are you?" Julie's voice was quaking, from surprise, from fear...and maybe something else. As he approached the bed, Johnny registered the eyes, the drugged expression, and he knew at once this would not be a cakewalk.

"I'm working for your father," Johnny told her simply. "I've come to take you home."

It took a moment for the meaning of his words to penetrate the mental fog, and then the lady's whole expression changed, surprise and fear melting beneath the sudden tears as she attempted to come off the bed and reach for him.

She stumbled in the process, but Johnny caught her, pulled her upright, pressed one damp cheek against his shoulder.

She was saying something, thanking him and clinging to him like a lost child who has finally found a friend amid a world of hostile strangers. Johnny Bolan heard her with a portion of his mind, but he was thinking through the next phase of their problem now, the final phase...one that was most likely to result in sudden, violent death.

The lady's captors would not give her up without a fight and he had no idea what the odds were at the moment. Half a dozen guns or half a hundred. Anything was possible inside the mammoth whorehouse.

He was so occupied with charting their escape route in his mind that Johnny almost missed the sound of footsteps just outside the door.

Almost.

He pivoted to find the bedroom door already swinging open, shattered locking mechanism useless now. Two hulking goons stood in the doorway staring at him, one with key in hand, the hand outstretched and suspended in midair.

"Well, ain't this cozy," Mr. Keys said when he found his tongue. "The bitch has company."

His smile froze Johnny Bolan to the marrow.

And he was still smiling when the men made their move.

21

Cherry Gifford gently pushed the bald man's groping hand away, wriggling to her feet. He looked so shocked and almost hurt that she bent over and let him have a glimpse of cleavage as she stroked his cheek.

"I'll be right back," she promised, smiling. "Just a sec', now, while I freshen up."

"You're fresh enough right now," he said, leering.

"Oh, no. Not nearly."

She was out of range before he had a chance to drag her back down on the couch. It took a moment to regain her bearings, then she struck out for the stairs across a shifting obstacle course composed of bodies in varied stages of undress.

The downstairs group-grope was about to hit its stride, she knew, and it would be the perfect cover for the move she had in mind. At any rate, it was the only cover she was likely to receive.

It had been simple getting in, despite the security that hung around Club Venus. A simple call to one of Cherry's friends who worked the joint three nights a week, the transfer of some cash she had received from Frank La-Mancha, and Cherry was in. The houseman never blinked an eye when she explained that she was substituting for one of the regulars.

She reached the stairs, glanced back around the room to see if anyone was watching her, and started up. If she was stopped she would just have to improvise—the ladies' room, a summons from the boss—whatever came to mind.

But Cherry guessed that one girl would not be missed in the orgy shaping up downstairs.

Except, perhaps, by the bald man from Dallas.

She had been in the club almost three hours now, more than long enough to satisfy herself that Julie Price was not downstairs among the working girls. If she was here at all, then she was on the second or third floor, or...

The idea that Julie was not even in Club Venus had been nagging Cherry from the moment she hatched her plan to infiltrate the place. It was a gamble, but the effort made her feel that she was being useful, doing something rather than just hiding out in some motel waiting for LaMancha's call.

She reached the second-floor landing and glanced each way along the corridor, disheartened by the line of silent, unmarked doors on either side. Another floor just like it lay above her, and she had no idea how she should proceed from here. And she sure could not start knocking on those doors and calling Julie Price's name. Not if she hoped to leave the club with life and limb intact.

She had decided that the safest method would be to work her way along the corridor and test each door in turn to see if it was locked. The open rooms could be examined and dismissed, assuming they were all unoccupied, and she could take her time in working out an angle of attack for any she found locked.

She flipped a mental coin, the left hand won, and she was veering off in that direction when a piercing scream came down to her from somewhere overhead. Before she could react or try to get a fix on the precise location of the sound, it was eclipsed by booming gunfire.

JOHNNY STRAIGHT-ARMED JULIE PRICE, propelling her away from him across the room. The KG-99 was in his hand, the muzzle rising, sweeping into target acquisition, and in front of him the goons were reacting with the swift reflexive movements of professionals.

The keyman dropped his ring while digging for a handgun that he carried almost front and center in a belly rig designed for speed. He had the chrome revolver in his hand and was already dropping into a shooting stance when Johnny Bolan fired.

The parabellum round had been intended for his target's chest, but the guy had crouched, avoiding death by inches. The bullet grazed his ear instead, and carried half of it away before it drilled his comrade through the solar plexus, pinning him against the doorjamb.

Johnny fired again, the 99's report ringing painfully inside his skull. An even louder roar, the houseman's cannon, and a hot wind fanned his cheek before he had a chance to roll toward the bed, still firing.

At the periphery of his vision Johnny saw his target reeling under the impact of the second round. His starched white shirtfront was spurting crimson now, and he was rocking back against the man behind him, both wounded gunners sprawling through the doorway and into the corridor beyond.

Johnny followed them grimly and aimed for the head as he pumped two more rounds into each twitching form. It was precaution time, and he could not afford to leave two wounded soldiers at his back while he was fighting for his life. For Julie Price. . . for the memory of Sandy Darlow.

Julie was staring at him from the far side of the room, where he had pushed her just before the guns went off. Her eyes were wide with shock as she took in the corpses, but whatever they were feeding her to keep her docile seemed to be preventing her from lapsing all the way into hysteria.

"We have to go," he told her flatly. "Right now."

She nodded weakly, did not move, and Johnny crossed the room to take her arm and steer her out around the crumpled bodies of the hardmen in the doorway.

Farther down the hall doors were opening, a tousled head emerging here and there to seek the sounds of gunfire, ducking back at the sight of Johnny Bolan with his KG-99 in hand. The customers would be no problem, he surmised, but there might be security on every floor, and they could spring upon him anywhere en route to the stairs.

Their exit could become a gantlet if the defenders of Club Venus reacted swiftly enough to seal off the upper floors.

And that increased the urgency of moving now, before the opposition had a chance to pull itself together and shake off the party mood.

Johnny guided his companion down the corridor, encouraged when she pulled her arm away from him and took his hand instead. The lady was recovering, and while she had a long way to go yet, she was getting there.

And Johnny Bolan hoped that she would have a chance to make it all the way.

They were already at the landing when he heard the sound of running feet below, now climbing, heading straight for their position. Eyes skimming back along the corridor, he knew they did not have the time to check each door until they found an open bedroom. Even if the first one clicked they would be run to ground.

No, he would take his chances in the open.

Hurriedly, he pushed the lady back and out of line with the staircase, preparing to meet the first charge alone. He counted but a single person closing, and there was a chance that they could pass this first obstruction without taking casualty of their own.

He stepped to the head of the stairs, the KG-99 braced in both hands submachine-gun style. Sighting downrange, his finger tensed on the trigger as he lined his sights up...on the face of an attractive, startled woman.

MACK BOLAN SLIPPED in through the kitchen service entrance and found himself alone. By the sounds that issued from beyond connecting doors, he guessed that members of the club were more inclined to drink their supper . . . or to snort it, possibly, through rolled-up, hundred-dollar bills.

He was grateful that he seemed to have arrived on orgy night instead of during some elaborate banquet when the kitchen would be overcrowded.

He was inside now, undetected, and he felt the numbers running, right, compelling him to seek the contact that had lured him here. He had to find the girl, and equally important, if not more so, was his need to find the Iceman.

Bobby Benedetto had a lot to answer for, damn right, and Bolan was about to hand his mark the check. But first he had to find him, make sure that no blameless flesh was in the way.

The Executioner left the kitchen, walked into a formal dining room—and found himself no longer alone. At the far end of a massive table, a man and woman stripped to the essentials were immersed in each other to the point that they were unconscious of his entry to the room. He left them to it, slipping out without disturbing them, his combat senses homing on the sounds of the main event in progress.

And he found it in what seemed to be a giant family room, with love seats, sofas and a host of padded easy chairs arranged like little islands in the middle of the floor. Each small oasis seemed to have its clique of occupants, with stragglers still drifting here and there among the groups, inspecting each in turn and searching for a stimulus to suit their needs.

He stopped his head count when he hit the seventies and realized that these were not the people he would need to be concerned about. He marked a houseman, two, a third . . . still dressed and hanging back around the fringes of the action. It was the gunners he would have to watch, and Bolan wondered how many others might be salted out of view around the house, the grounds, just waiting to respond in case of an alarm.

No matter how much juice he carried with the local

government, the Iceman would have taken out insurance at another level, making damned sure that his guests, his girls, his property were safe and sound and under guard. He would not trust police, no matter how well paid a few of them might be, to look the other way, and he could not afford to trust his fellow cannibals beyond the limits of his vision, either.

And there would be more than just these three guns, Bolan knew it with a certainty that turned his eyes to ice behind the mask of combat paint.

He was already scanning for a pathway through the crush of florid flesh when gunshots sounded somewhere on a floor above. A faint sound, muffled by the distance, by the walls, by the stereo that pulsed with tribal rhythms in a corner of the room, but unmistakable, for all of that.

The housemen were reacting, first one, then the others, grouping and moving off in the direction of the stairs. As Bolan watched, a side door opened across the room and half a dozen more tuxedos suddenly emerged, some of them pawing inside their coats for hardware.

So someone had begun the grim festivities without him.

Fair enough.

But there was no rule on the books forbidding entry of a tardy player to the game, and Bolan slipped from cover like a gliding shadow in the muted lighting of the orgy room. He held the Uzi ready as he fell in behind the palace guards, pursuing them around the wide perimeter of the chamber.

Another burst of semiautomatic fire, and it was closer now, as if the gunner had come down a floor between engagements. Bolan's frown was etched into his face as he sped up, intent on closing with the firing squad as soon as possible.

Half a dozen of them were already on the stairs, guns out, heading toward the landing on the second floor.

Bolan hurdled straining, writhing bodies in his haste until he reached the staircase. He saw his opposition poised above him on the landing, several of them crouching and angling weapons toward a target still beyond his line of sight.

Whoever might be up there, drawing fire and now returning it, he needed help.

The Executioner was sprinting up the staircase three steps at a time before the flankers sensed his presence, turned and saw him coming for them like a specter out of hell. And he was scarcely thirty feet away when one and then another opened fire.

TIM BRADDOCK TOOK A LAST DRAG on his cigarette and flicked it out the window of his unmarked cruiser, watching as the ember arced through darkness and exploded into sparks on contact with the pavement. Grudgingly, aware that it was still too soon, he checked his watch for perhaps the hundredth time.

Beside him, Benny Kelso, his lieutenant, shifted in his seat and expelled a weary sigh.

"I'd say that everybody's in."

"Not yet."

It wasn't time, and Braddock was determined not to jump the gun on this one.

"Well, maybe if we all knew just exactly what we're waiting for..."

Oh, sure. And Braddock could have used a little certainty in that regard himself.

"You're waiting for the word," he said at last, and that provoked another sigh from Kelso as he settled back into his seat.

On the phone Mack Bolan had not gone into all the fine specifics when he sketched his plan. He needed cops, and plenty of them, at Club Venus, but they must not put in an appearance prior to eleven o'clock. That left Braddock with almost ten minutes to kill, and the search warrant was burning a hole in his pocket already.

It had been something of a task to get the warrant. This Benedetto character had purchased insulation from the top, but with a little planning, Braddock finally turned a rookie judge who had been overlooked by Mr. Money-bags. Beyond that, it was just a matter of convincing the court that he had probable cause to suspect assorted felonies in progress, and the deal was set.

Except that he had felt compelled to detail officers to watch his rookie judge and make damned certain that the club's proprietor was not tipped off before the raid.

And there had been the matter of his own troops. Tim Braddock had been forced to handpick members of the raiding party. He did not suspect a single member of his team, but there was no damn point in taking any chances.

And now they were together, on site, waiting.

For the word.

He would be giving it, whatever happened, at eleven sharp. If Bolan's business was completed, if he was still in there, even if the damned guy never showed at all, the raid was coming off on time.

Tim Braddock meant to keep his promise.

He wondered what might happen if the Executioner had been delayed, if he was still at work inside when they came crashing through the wide front doors. He knew the guy had never fired on cops before, suspected that he never would, but that would not prevent the members of Tim Braddock's handpicked team from getting in some target practice of their own.

He did not want to cause Bolan's death, but he could not protect the soldier if he hung around and let the SWAT team find him inside Club Venus. They were loaded up for bear, expecting trouble, and at any sign of armed resistance there would be a need for coroners at the lush estate.

The Homicide detective wished Mack Bolan well and checked his watch again. Eight minutes now, and counting down.

Another hour or so, and he would have eleven days remaining on the job. Providing he survived the hour that lay in front of him.

And if it all went sour, somehow, well, at least Tim Braddock knew that he had tried to get it right this one last time. He would not feel that the night, the past years were wasted.

He felt more alive right now, the captain realized, than he had at any time in years. And since he had lost his wife a few years back, he had been going through the motions, not exactly sloughing off, but never going for that extra yardage, either.

Like tonight.

If Bolan kept his end up—even if he failed, somehow—the Venus raid was going to provide a major upset for the status quo around L.A. and Hollywood. The thought made Braddock smile, and he was well aware there would not be a better chance to get his last licks in within the next eleven days.

It would be good to turn the flat rock over and reveal what went on underneath. And if some celebrity assholes got scorched by the heat, why, so much the better.

The sergeant's words came back at him from Hotel Hell. "Somebody really oughta give this place an enema."

And this was where the nozzle went, damned right.

Another...what...six minutes now? Then Braddock would be turning on the tap. After that, it would be every turd for himself.

He settled back into his seat, trying to relax and knowing it was hopeless. Another cigarette might help, and he was fishing for the pack when high-beam headlights stabbed him in the eyes. A limo turned square into the middle of their stakeout, flanked by several others.

Braddock stopped counting on the fifth car, forgot about the smoke as he sat bolt upright in his seat, already reaching for his gun on instinct. At his side, Lieutenant

Kelso had a hand out, groping for the two-way radio, but Braddock seized his wrist, prevented him from reaching it.

"Not yet," he snapped. "It isn't time."

"Well, what the hell—"

"Another second now, relax. It won't be long."

Not long. But he was sweating now, despite the cool night breeze that wafted through his open window. The combination of perspiration and wind produced a chill that raised gooseflesh on his back and arms. The captain shivered and locked his fingers tight around the holstered revolver as if to stop himself from trembling.

Not long now, he told himself.

Not long.

22

"Hey, relax!"

The lady froze with both arms out, palms open, as if flesh and bone could block the rounds from Johnny Bolan's KG-99. He glanced down the stairs, saw no one on her heels, and eased off the trigger.

"I hope you're looking for the powder room," he told her, wondering what he would do, and knowing in his heart that he would have no choice if she turned out to be an enemy.

"The fact is, I've been looking high and low around this dump for her."

She was pointing past Johnny toward the spot where Julie Price had reemerged from cover when she heard the other woman's voice.

"How's that?"

He heard the numbers running in his mind, a timer counting down to doomsday, but he did not dare proceed until he had some rough idea of what the hell was going on. This wild card might be their salvation, or their death, and either way he had to get a feel for her before he took her in or left her living at his back.

The lady was beside him now, no longer looking at his weapon, and from where she stood the bodies huddled in the corridor downrange were plainly visible.

"I don't think you've got time to hear my whole biography," she said. "I'm working with a guy named Frank LaMancha, and we've both been through the wringer looking for your shadow there."

The name hit Johnny Bolan like a fist above the heart and sent his pulse pounding in his ears.

LaMancha.

Mack!

And sure, the lady's voice was more than just a little bit familiar. If he concentrated, put her on the telephone...

She stepped around him, moving close to Julie Price.

"Are you all right, kid? You remember me? It's Cherry."

"Cherry."

There was precious little recognition in the tone, and Johnny did not have the time to stretch out their reunion. There were voices on the stairs below, and it sounded like a hunting party.

"Time to go," he told the women. "We've got company below."

"What did you have in mind?" the new arrival asked.

"We haven't got a lot of options," Johnny answered. "One way down as far as I know."

They were halfway to the second-floor landing when Johnny spied the pointman of the hunting party emerging into view with one hand on the banister, the other wrapped around an Army-issue .45. The two men saw each other simultaneously, and the gunner blurted out a wordless warning to the others, snapping up his weapon as he tried to find a crouch.

There was a split-second lapse between the shots, but Johnny got there first, squeezing off a deadly triple-punch before the Army Colt erupted with its single, deadly word. The incoming round gouged plaster somewhere to his left, milking a scream out of Julie, but his target was staggering, falling, the impact of the manglers taking all the starch out in a single sweep.

Johnny rushed the landing, pumping more rounds downstairs at random, knowing there would be no hope if his opponents came at them en masse. Assorted handguns were unloading on him from below, and someone down there had a shotgun, raining buckshot on the walls and ceiling.

They were at an impasse, Johnny knew, which must not last. The troops downstairs could seal them off and starve them out, if necessary, waiting in their relative security until the two invaders had exhausted all their ammunition, rushing them when they were tired or unprepared. It only took one man to hold the stairs against an army, and if the army could not come up, neither could the little Bolan force get downstairs to his waiting car and freedom.

But Johnny had not come to die inside Club Venus.

"I need some cover, Cherry. Can you use this?" he asked, tossing her an automatic pistol.

Her eyes went wide for just a heartbeat, and her voice was worried when she answered him.

"The odds are lousy, guy."

"They don't get any better."

"Yeah, I see your point. You've got your cover."

Johnny hesitated, glancing back at Julie Price before his eyes returned to Cherry. "Guess I didn't thank you for the tip."

"What tip?" It hit her then, and recognition brought a little sheepish smile. "Oh, wow. The phone guy."

Johnny nodded.

"From the looks of things, I could've saved the dime."

"Maybe next time. You ready?"

She gripped the little automatic in both hands and nodded silently.

He pushed off, rolling out of cover, keeping low as weapons opened on him from below, at the midpoint of the stairs. A number of the hostiles had been climbing quietly to seek a better vantage point, and Johnny caught them unprepared as he started squeezing off rapid-fire. He saw one buckle, then another, and the girl was firing down at them now, winging one as he sprinted for safety. The rest were homing on their muzzle flashes, picking up the range, when something unexpected happened to distract them.

At the bottom of the stairs, a submachine gun joined the party, stingers ripping through the hunters from behind and toppling a pair of them before they realized that they were suddenly surrounded. From his lookout post, Johnny saw a ghostly black-clad figure charging in among the few survivors of the hunting party, chopping at them with short bursts from his Uzi as he cut off their retreat. Another moment, and the stairs were littered with their bodies, nothing left between Johnny Bolan and his brother but the dead.

And Cherry recognized the Executioner before he had a chance to make it halfway up the stairs. A startled cry of "Frank," and she let fall the smoking pistol, already moving toward the stairs, her arms outstretched to greet him.

The bullet struck her just behind the ear, pitching her forward with sufficient force to clear the railing and plummet a dozen feet to a rolling impact with the stairs. She came to rest against Mack Bolan's legs, but Johnny never saw her fall. He was too busy pivoting to face the enemy behind them.

Four men, three with tuxedos on the firing line... and bringing up the rear an apparition in midnight leather, ghastly with the mask of a medieval torturer pulled down across his face.

Another time he might have laughed and changed the channel, but the younger Bolan was too busy firing now, his bullets chopping down the tallest of the three tuxedos, drilling through another's shoulder, spinning him around and throwing him against the ghoul in leather. Weapons were unloading on him now, the bullets eating plaster inches overhead. And it was over now, he knew that he was dead—

Except that suddenly his brother was beside him on the landing, Uzi rattling in concert with the barking of his

KG-99. The two remaining housemen were crumpling, an abstract outline of their dying etched into the wall by spattered blood and bullet scars.

The man in leather was agile, Johnny had to give him that. Before the Bolan guns could come to bear on his position he had raced across the hall and ducked into an alcove where a Grecian statue kept its lonely vigil. And as the brothers watched, amazed, he kept going through the wall, which pivoted on hidden hinges, opening to let him pass. A burst from Bolan's chopper took the statue's face off, but the target was already out of sight.

Mack turned back to Johnny. "Are you hit?"

The younger Bolan shook his head.

"All right," the Executioner continued, glancing at his watch. "You have a minute and a half to get your package out of here before the law drops in. East wall, midway."

He was feeding a new magazine into the Uzi's pistol grip, already moving toward the alcove where the leather man had disappeared.

"Hey, wait," the younger Bolan called. "The joint's a write-off. Why not let the stragglers go?"

"This straggler's why I came," his brother answered.

And a heartbeat later he was gone.

VINCE ANDRIOLA CHECKED THE LOAD on his revolver, snapped it shut and thrust it back into the waistband of his slacks. The soldiers flanking him and the two facing him from drop-down jump seats, carried loaded riot shotguns and carbines.

He would teach Bobby Benedetto a lesson, and any other misbegotten sons of bitches who had rallied to his cause against their *capo*.

Andriola smiled to mask his nervousness, and one of the gunners sitting opposite returned the grin. He wondered how these men could look so goddamned casual when they were on the way to the biggest killing party any of them had ever seen. It magnified his fear, somehow, to see that others did not seem to be afraid.

But he was leading the troops, and that was what would matter when the smoke had cleared away. They would remember he was with them in the forefront of the battle, and the word would spread—throughout his Family at first, and then to others.

He might become a holy legend if he wasn't careful, Andriola thought, and now the smile was broader, more sincere.

They cleared the final corner and his driver took them into the street where Benedetto had his club. The wrought-iron gates hove into view ahead, the gate man pacing back and forth.

Andriola felt the driver slowing into the approach, and he leaned forward, resting one hand on the wheelman's shoulder, squeezing hard.

"Don't stop," he ordered gruffly.

"But the gates—"

"The gates, my ass. Go through the gates!"

"Yes, sir."

Acceleration pushed him back into the seat cushions as they surged forward, tires scorching asphalt. The Lincoln rocked into a right-hand turn, barreling toward impact with the broad double gates. He braced himself and caught a glimpse of the gate man hightailing it for cover.

They hit the gates dead center, met a brief resistance from the lock, and then continued through, the wrought-iron panels folding out before them like garage doors, dragging across the Lincoln's hood and roof as they passed underneath.

Andriola's pulse was hammering inside his head, and now he had the short revolver in his fist again. Behind him, the other cars were rumbling through the sagging gates, finally bulling them out of the way.

"We got company," the driver barked, his eyes wide in the rearview mirror.

Andriola craned around, staring past the other cars in his motorcade toward the flashing red and yellow lights of the police cars that were following. And instantly he knew it was a setup. Bobby "Smart-Ass" Benedetto had just suckered him into a trap.

"What should we do, boss?"

The question came from a gunner on his left, and the guy didn't look so damned content now.

"What do we do? What do you think we do?" the *capo* of Los Angeles responded bitterly. "We got a job, and I don't care how many cops this Benedetto calls. We take him out. We take 'em *all*!"

TIM BRADDOCK HAD THE MICROPHONE in hand before the lead car in the caravan broke through the gates.

"It's going down!" he told the troops arranged around Club Venus in a ring of steel. "Move in. *Move in!*"

And Braddock fired the engine in his unmarked cruiser, flooring the pedal as they smoked out of there and fell in line behind the Mafia motorcade.

"What is this shit?" Lieutenant Kelso asked, already wrestling the shotgun free of dashboard mounts.

"This is the payoff," Braddock told him enigmatically.

They cleared the gates and were running close up on the last crew wagon's tail before the first SWAT vehicle appeared in Braddock's rearview, lights and siren cranking into high. It felt better with an army at his back, but he was still out front, and it looked as if they were racing square into the middle of a war zone.

For just a moment, Braddock wondered what Mack Bolan could have done this time to turn the Family in upon itself. No matter, really, just as long as it paid off.

Except that he was early by some two minutes. And he wondered if the Executioner had had the time he needed to complete his job inside. . .or if he ever made it to the club at all.

There had been none of the accustomed fireworks, but the goddamned place was more than likely soundproofed, come to think of it. An army could be dying on the inside, and you would not know it sitting in the flower garden.

Ahead, the limousines were fanning out, three of them veering off the drive to run abreast of the point car, racing toward the house and chewing up a wide expanse of lawn.

"Keep on 'em!" Kelso blurted, caught up in the chase, and Braddock kept the hammer down, nosing in behind his quarry in the lead car.

Andriola would be in the Lincoln if he was here at all, and the Homicide captain was reserving that one for himself. Whoever walked away from this encounter, he meant for Andriola to remember it for a while.

The limos had begun to slow, the lead car sluing right, then left as the driver stood on his brakes. The tanks came to rest in a tight semicircle, all facing the steps and front door of Club Venus, their high beams lighting up the manor house. Men were piling out of the crew wagons racking shells into shotguns and carbines, a few of them turning back to face the squad cars, most of them concentrating on the primary target.

Braddock slammed on the brakes, and then they were unloading, Braddock clawing for the Diamondback .38 that he wore on his hip. Thirty yards away, a gunner had his carbine up and aimed in their direction, but Kelso hit him with the 12-gauge charge and dropped him backward.

A smattering of fire erupted from the house, but it was weak at best. The solid wall of fire returned by Andriola's men exploded windows, riddled doors and whittled at the brickwork, silencing the inner guns before they had a chance to find the range.

Behind Tim Braddock, SWAT-team members were unloading by the numbers, fanning out to take up their positions at the rear of Andriola's troops. Their chief was bawling for a cease-fire through his bullhorn, but the cannibals weren't buying it. No sooner had they finished riddling Club Venus from the front than they were turning back to face the challenge at their back.

The captain winced as firing opened up on both sides of the line, but he was waiting, watching, when a small form hunched against the firestorm wriggled from the lead car, seeking better cover. Braddock tracked *Don* Andriola with his Diamondback, leading the shadow target slightly, allowing for the darkness and his own excitement.

Another second now, you bastard. One more step.

And he was smiling when he squeezed the trigger.

THE STAIRS LED DOWNWARD into darkness, and Mack Bolan followed slowly, cautiously, along the Iceman's track. The Uzi probed ahead of him, a lethal blind man's cane, prepared to answer any challenge with a stream of parabellum manglers that would need no target in the confines of the stairwell.

Bolan cursed himself for letting Benedetto slip away. There might not be a second chance to take him now before he went to ground or made his way out of the city.

If Benedetto got away, then he would wait. Come back, if necessary, as many times as it might take to do the job.

There would be no free pass for Bobby Benedetto, not while Bolan lived. The Iceman's tab was overdue, with too much interest in arrears to simply let it go.

He owed the man in leather, right. For Julie Price. For all the others he had brutalized and victimized along the way.

And now, for Cherry Gifford.

She was riding on the Bolan conscience, sure, another friendly ghost among. . . how many?

Stop it, now!

A moment of distraction would be all it took to get himself killed, and Bolan could not well afford to die before he locked his hands around the Iceman's throat and watched the fear of death check in behind those soulless eyes.

Twenty feet or so below him, the soldier glimpsed a razor-thin line of feeble light...the outline of a doorway at the bottom of the stairs. Despite the urge to run, he slowed his pace deliberately, aware that Benedetto could be waiting for him on the other side.

When Bolan reached his destination, he could see that the door was partially ajar—and it was not a door in the accepted sense. A portal, right, but it had been disguised in such a way that there was no apparent knob, no visible hinges...nothing but a chunk of wall that revolved slowly outward under his hand.

He went through in a shoulder roll and came up on his knees, the Uzi sweeping back and forth in search of a nonexistent target. Concrete floor, the smell of gasoline and oil told Bolan instantly that he was in a small garage. His entryway had been disguised by shelving, thrown wide now and standing open on the black rectangle of the stairwell.

Also standing open, Bolan saw, was the main door of the garage. He reached it in a loping run just in time to see the taillights of a sports car winking around the first curve of a narrow track that ran among the trees.

The Iceman had prepared a back door for himself, of course. And he was out of there, away and running free toward...what?

Mack Bolan knew the answer suddenly, instinctively, as if it had been written on the wall in words of fire. He knew where he could find the Iceman, but he would have to get there, somehow, without wasting the precious moments it would take to find his wheels.

Then he saw it. Hell, the fates must be riding with him this night, he thought.

The motorcycle stood against a wall of the garage, its key in the ignition. Benedetto's backup system, sure, in case the car malfunctioned. Bolan thanked the universe for his opponent's thorough paranoia as he climbed aboard, the Uzi slung across his back, and kicked the engine into life.

He had a chance.
Just that, and nothing more.
But it would have to do, damn right.
The Executioner was out of miracles.

23

The Iceman's big Topanga Canyon studio was not ablaze with lights on Bolan's second visit in as many days. The troops were learning slowly, and they would not make it easy for him this time.

Which was fine with Bolan, sure.

He had surmised that his target would not run directly home. The Venus raid would raise a blistering heat, and it would ultimately ring in Benedetto's name as owner of the property. He would be sought for questioning, at least, by several different law-enforcement agencies, and he was not the type to let himself be taken unprepared. There would be lawyers to consult—if they had not been bagged already by police—and Benedetto might decide to take a short vacation, finally surrender at his leisure with a plea of ignorance to anything that happened while he was "away on business."

It was a classic move played out each year by a thousand different hoods and crooked businessmen from coast to coast. Sometimes it worked. Sometimes the judge and jury were persuaded by a choirboy face and gift of gab, convinced by pleas of gullibility or plain stupidity. Sometimes.

But not this time.

The Executioner spent precious numbers circling the house, inside the cover of the trees, experiencing tightness in his gut at the first sight of the sports car parked in back. When he was finished, he had marked the sentries. . . five in all. . . and had registered their individual positions in his mind. They had been placed strategically, but they were weak in numbers, and despite their greater caution they were still unused to jungle warfare Bolan-style.

When he had the entrances and exits firmly in his mind, he started working back along the circuit with garrotes, with tempered steel, with crushing hands. He took them five-for-five without a sound, and when he finished he was all alone outside the rambling studio.

Alone with death and darkness.

It was judgment night for Bobby Benedetto, and the Executioner was ready to present the bastard with his tab.

The doors were locked, predictably, but they had never been designed for keeping out determined pros, and Bolan made his entry through the broad French doors that fronted a flagstone patio. He found himself inside a one-time family room, almost devoid of furniture and clearly seldom used. Whereas Club Venus was a playground, this place had the earmarks of a factory, and Bolan guessed that Benedetto's workers did their resting mainly when they lay down, nude, in front of movie cameras.

The silver AutoMag was in his fist as Bolan scanned the family room, moved on to the adjacent kitchen with its pantry, found them empty. He backtracked through the living room, proceeding toward the double doors directly opposite—and almost stumbled over Bobby Benedetto as the guy emerged, valise in hand.

He was preparing to evacuate, and the little smile became a grimace as he caught sight of Bolan. He gave a strangled cry as Bolan raised the AutoMag, already sighting in, and Benedetto spun around, his satchel snagging on the door, discarded in his haste to get away.

The mighty .44 bucked and roared, 240 grains of death impacting inches from the Iceman's head and punching out a fist-sized peephole in the door. A yelp of pain as flying splinters stung the Iceman's cheek, and then he disappeared.

The Executioner pursued him through the double doors

and found himself inside a chamber straight out of the *Arabian Nights*, complete with tapestries on the walls, a clump of rubberized palmettos and a bed of giant cushions on the floor. It was a sound stage, right, with lights suspended from the open beams above his head, but Bolan's full attention focused on the starring player in his script.

The Iceman had been grappling with a hidden door when Bolan entered, but he gave it up at once, a little blubbering sob his only sound before he turned and leaped, headfirst, directly *through* the opposite wall.

It was a canvas mock-up, and Bolan understood at once how a conventional Topanga Canyon pleasure palace had become a studio where dreams—and nightmares—were translated into celluloid reality. He crouched and risked a shot at Benedetto through the makeshift exit, fanning painted canvas with the wind of death, rewarded as the Iceman stumbled, reeling, clutching his side.

The next set might have been an ordinary office but for all the Nazi flags and reproduction portraits of the führer on the wall. A corner to Bolan's right was piled with other, folded flags, and there were likenesses of Castro, Idi Amin, the Ayatollah...all the trappings for a change of scene, depending on the mood of the director. Whips and shackles banished any thought of this place being used for casual interviews.

The Iceman was intent on battering a doorway through the canvas wall, his efforts leaving blood smears on the tarp. Bolan helped him get there with a screaming Magnum round that ripped his shoulder from its socket and propelled him facefirst through the flimsy barricade.

The Executioner stepped through behind his wounded quarry and emerged into a mock-up dungeon that reminded him of something from a Vincent Price movie. But otherwise the place was perfect, right down to the rack at center stage, the brazier full of charcoal—cool now—with the shafts of pokers rising out of it like candles on some grisly birthday cake. The walls were fitted with hanging shackles that appeared to be the genuine article, and Bolan sensed that they had reached the end of one wing in the studio. The Iceman would not be escaping through the walls this time—assuming that he had the strength to stand.

And Bolan's quarry, so far, was content with wriggling across the dark linoleum like some misshapen reptile, trailing blood where his hands and knees had smeared it like a giant's finger paint. He reached the rack and started slowly, painfully, hauling himself erect while Bolan watched, a portion of his mind still checking out the set.

They had been filming here, and recently—perhaps the very night that Bolan liberated Foster Price.

A moment's searching found the light switch, and he hit the kliegs, illuminating Benedetto in a sudden noonday blaze. The mafioso raised his one good arm to shield his eyes and almost lost his balance in the process. He found the Executioner through squinting eyes and spent another moment searching for his voice beneath the pain.

And it was long enough for Bolan to assess his shot.

Bobby Benedetto's lips were working, soundlessly at first, but gradually his voice emerged, a cracked falsetto.

"Hey, man . . . we can work it out, believe me. Anything you want. Just name it, huh?"

The Executioner stared back at him without emotion, finally spoke.

"So, give it to me like you mean it."

"What? Oh . . . right." The monster saw a gleam of hope behind the klieg lights. "Listen, I've got contacts. Hell, you must know that. Just say the word, I'll line you up with any kinda action you can handle."

Life was running out of him, but Benedetto could not give up. The breathless voice rasped on.

"You like some coke? I'll set you up a mountain of it, man . . . all prime Colombian. Want money? Name your price."

And something clicked behind the wounded ferret's eyes, a circuit closing as he reached down deep for something that would buy him back his life.

"I bet you like the ladies, huh? So, how about a harem, man, what say? Some nice young chicken, maybe...."

Bolan felt his insides turning over, fury spilling out of him along the raised extension of his gun arm. Benedetto saw the cannon swinging onto target, knew, somehow, that he had gone too far, and there was only time to raise his hand, to scream in helpless terror, before the big warrior opened fire.

The Magnum emptied in rapid-fire, its five rounds lifting Bobby Benedetto off his feet, propelling him across the rack and out of frame.

Bolan experienced a fleeting calm as he turned his back on the mock dungeon and its lifeless prisoner.

Meet

Don Pendleton

and the

Mack Bolan, Able Team, Phoenix Force, Track and SOBs writing teams

at the
world's first
Mack Bolan Convention,
The San Franciscan Hotel
(Market & 8th at the Civic Center)

Sunday, May 26th, 1985

Weapons • Posters Videos • Memorabilia Cover art • Buy and Sell Briefings

Watch for ads in your daily newspaper for information on this long-awaited event, or write to: **Gold Eagle Books**, Reader Management, P.O. Box 80718, Las Vegas, NV 89180

DON PENDLETON'S EXECUTIONER

MACK BOLAN

Sergeant Mercy in Nam.. The Executioner in the Mafia
Wars... Colonel John Phoenix in the Terrorist Wars....
Now Mack Bolan fights his loneliest war! You've never
read writing like this before. By fire and maneuver, Bolan
will rack up hell in a world shock-tilted by terror. He
wages unsanctioned war—everywhere!

GOLD
EAGLE

GET THE NEW WAR BOOK AND MACK BOLAN BUMPER STICKER FREE!

Mail this coupon today!

Mack Bolan is a Winner!

Readers everywhere applaud his success.

"You deserve some kind of reward for delivering such reading pleasure to millions of people throughout the world."

M.L., *Chicago, Illinois*

"Bolan isn't a killer—he is a positive force fighting the degeneration of man. He is also awesomely entertaining, as fine a literary hero as any."

S.S., Augsburg, Germany

"I want to congratulate you on your decision to put our Sergeant into the fight against terrorism. With the world situation today, it will endear many more people to this man of courage."

B.C., New York, New York

"I am in the army, and I would be proud to serve with Mack Bolan and cover his back down the first mile, and second, and third if he said it was needed."

P.E.D., APO, New York

"I think my Executioner collection is the finest thing I own, or probably ever will own."

R.C., Gainesville, Florida

*Names available on request.